I0618182

# Blackwater Creek

## By Donna R Brown

ISBN-10: 0615961819
ISBN-13: 978-0615961811

# Acknowledgements

To my parents, Weldon and Edie Jones, for always believing in me and to my Mom in particular for your endless hours of formatting, editing and revising. I could never have done it without you. To my daughter, Amanda Burlin and my dearest friends, Doug and Beth Banks, for the fruitful brainstorming sessions and your inspiring ideas. To my brother, Sergeant Steve Jones, for your encouragement and for always sharing my love of reading, in childhood and still today. To my Aunt Shirley for being so *Shirley*, and to my Aunt Glenda for all your support.

My love and gratitude for the people of Liberty, Texas, my inspiration for the town of Blackwater. In particular I'd like to thank Jax Hamburgers, as you will always be my Ladybird Café.

And last but not least, to my husband, Tim, for being the love of my life, and for loving me in return.

Above all, to my Father in heaven to Whom I owe all gratitude for giving His Son. I have been truly blessed.

# Chapter 1

Ludie saw the iced tea glass teetering on the tray her friend was carrying and lunged toward it, missing by a split second. The sound of glass shattering disrupted lunch for all the locals of Blackwater, Texas who were eating at the Ladybird Café. Shards of glass scattered across the floor, the harsh lights of the diner reflecting on the stainless steel walls. Mavis, the hands-down best waitress in town according to many, and the longest employed according to fact, nearly slipped in the pool of tea that was spreading rapidly across the floor. Within seconds of the calamity, most everyone had gone back to their conversations and resumed eating lunch as though nothing had happened.

"Looks like I got here just in time. What happened?" Ludie asked while looking up from the largest pieces of broken glass she was attempting to pick up. "You can balance a tray in your sleep."

Mavis smiled in response, her attention focused on the front of her pink uniform and apron. Ketchup, tea and honey-mustard dressing that had splattered from the dishes on the tray created an abstract art-work of her attire. "I don't know," she said weakly. "Just clumsy, I guess. I'm glad you're here." She thanked Ludie for her help and immediately set out to replace the drinks and items lost on the tray, re-ordering the plates that had fallen while her co-worker continued with the clean-up.

Ludie gasped, realizing she'd just sliced her finger on a sharp edge. She saw the blood rushing to the surface and quickly applied pressure. "Just a scratch," she yelled out to a concerned Mavis. "I guess you're not the only clumsy one," she laughed. "It's not bad. Let's pull ourselves together before Birdie comes out here to see what's going on."

A few minutes later Mavis brushed past her with two heavy-laden trays on her way to the table usually reserved for the town's politicians: the mayor, city councilmen, and a couple of school board members.

"You okay, Sweetheart?" Mavis asked her.

"Yes ma'am, it's already stopped bleeding." Ludie held up her bandaged index finger to show her.

"Good. I started out running behind this morning, and that little bit of chaos sure didn't help," she chuckled, craning her neck to peer out across the dining room.

"Why were you running behind? That's not like you."

"Nothing major," Mavis answered. "I just got distracted earlier and got off to a slow start." The distraction was no doubt Melvin, a confirmed member of the political table, regardless of the fact that he'd never served or been employed in city politics. He was a fixture in the town and always seemed to be a part of the conversation. Also, he seemed to consider himself the unofficial founder of the Mavis fan club. He watched her every move and cornered her at every opportunity to ask her for a date. Mavis was in her early seventies with a polished appearance, and she clearly paid attention to detail when she dressed every morning. Her silver-frosted nutmeg hair always looked like she'd just left the salon, neatly pinned up, with soft tendrils escaping as though it had been planned that way. The pink pencil tucked behind her ear completed her look as would any well-chosen accessory. Mavis had a slight matronly air about her, although she'd never had any children of her own. She picked up her glasses that were hanging from a beaded chain resting on her chest and put them on, focusing on her order pad. It wasn't as though she *had* to look. She got every order right, every time.

Ludie walked behind the counter, wrapping her apron strings around in front and tying them. Grabbing a full pot of fresh-brewed coffee, she began her rounds. She made her way first to the table claimed by the "good ole' boys," as they had been appropriately dubbed. That was one thing that could be said about Blackwater, Texas. Everyone involved in managing anything in town was a "good ole' boy." The first one to speak, of course, was Melvin.

"I thought Mavis was our waitress," he said, stretching his neck to catch sight of her.

"Relax, cowboy," Ludie smiled. "I'm only here to fill your coffee. I'll send her right over," she sang out, glancing back at a frowning Mavis over her shoulder. Spending so much time with Mavis and Birdie in the café' was comforting, as they were roughly the same age that Nanny would be, if she hadn't passed away. It was nice to be mothered and fussed over by these older ladies, and it even lessened the sting of losing Nanny a little.

When Ludie woke up the next morning she looked around her room and focused on her clock to make sure she hadn't overslept. She lived in Nanny and Poppa's farmhouse and daily found herself surrounded by memories, from the frilly curtains that hung on every window to the hand-made quilts that lay on every bed. Ludie fell asleep most nights to the quiet ticking of Nanny's beloved clocks on the wall lulling her to sleep, and she awoke to the crowing of Nanny's not-so-beloved roosters every morning. Knowing she had a few extra minutes, she snuggled down into her bed, prolonging the moment. She smiled when she thought of Nanny, and the important life's lessons she had learned at her hands.

"'*Vengeance is mine*,' saith the Lord." And Nanny. Ludie smiled at the memory. Nanny always had a saying for every occasion. Once, when Ludie was seven years old, Nanny had found her in the front yard collecting rocks from the gravel at the end of the driveway near the road into an old metal coffee can.

"What in heaven's name are you gonna' do with all those rocks?" she had asked, which gave Ludie a moment to reflect on how ridiculous her plan would sound. It had seemed like such a grand plan, but having to verbalize it made it

4

seem like child's play, which she supposed it was.

"Every day after school Natalie Broadway calls me 'Ludie Tootie Harelip' and throws rocks at me when I pass by her house on the way home. It hurts my legs!" And oh, how it hurt. Her bare long legs being pelted with showers of gravel had begun to wear on her. It was time to take action. She had relayed her plan of revenge to a disapproving Nanny, who'd wasted no time in setting her straight.

"You will do no such thing, young lady!" she said. "If she insists on being hateful, she's the one who'll have to face the Lord with it someday. But you're not gonna' lower yourself to her level." Nanny had made her remove all the little concrete weapons from the rusted coffee can and spread them back out across the driveway, all the while listening to her sage advice about the golden rule.

That night after everyone had gone to bed, Ludie had snuck out to the yard and began gathering her rocks all over again to prepare for her brilliant act of revenge. She knew she'd one day have to face the Lord, too, but it wouldn't be for years. Natalie, however, she would have to face tomorrow after school. Her plan had seemed perfect and would give the good Lord time to see what kind of person Natalie really was.

Frowning at the memory, Ludie threw back the covers and sat up, leaving her linens rumpled beneath her. Rising from bed, she stepped into her fuzzy pink slippers and padded down the stairs. She started some coffee brewing then stood at the kitchen window to look outside. Being in the kitchen reminded her so much of Nanny. She'd been gone a number of years now, but her sayings and advice lived on. Ludie was twenty-one now, and those painful events from the playground should be long gone from her memory, but they weren't. The scars of childhood remained as did the slightly visible scars from the surgery to correct her cleft palate. It wasn't as noticeable now, especially with the make-up Poppa had let her buy at the drug store when she'd started high school, but it was still there. He'd always made it clear that grandfathers didn't know much at all about makeup and other such girl things, but he'd been indulgent enough and usually trusted her to make prudent decisions. She'd never made him regret it, as she always applied her makeup lightly, blending it carefully to accentuate the contours of her face and conceal her scars.

The aroma of the fresh-brewed coffee drew her attention away from her reverie. She poured some and then stirred in some creamer. Taking her cup with her, she headed up the stairs to get dressed. When she was ready to start the day a short time later, she descended the stairs and glanced around to see if Poppa had come back inside. When she didn't see him, she went back into the kitchen to put her cup away.

"Poppa!" she called out to him, but got no reply. The house was quiet. She moved the curtains aside to check the backyard. At this time of morning he'd likely be in his workshop or gathering eggs. She stepped out onto the porch, letting the screen door slam behind her, quickly descended the porch steps and started across the yard. Wet grass clung to her boots, and she quietly cursed at herself for not taking the stone path. When she found him a few minutes later, he was in the hen house collecting eggs.

"Whatcha' need, Mouse?" He'd been calling her 'mouse' since she'd gotten her first pair of glasses in the second grade, not long after she'd become a gravel target. When she'd put the glasses on for the first time, resting at the bridge of her pointed little nose, Poppa had said she was the cutest little mouse he'd ever seen. It didn't help that her hair was classic mousy-brown. As for Poppa himself, he was the quintessential country grandfather. Ever since he'd retired from the refinery to work the farm full time, he'd gotten up every single morning before 6:00 am and put on his coveralls. His work ethic was strong, only his love for his granddaughter stronger. And here he was, gathering the eggs, just on time. *If he was ever more than a few minutes late*, Ludie thought, *the hens would worry.*

"Can't stay for breakfast," she said, eyeing one of the baskets of eggs.

"Am I taking these to Birdie?" she asked. "I can rinse them off and count them into cartons for you before I go."

"Nope, you go on ahead. I'll take these to her later." She gave him a quick kiss on the cheek and started back to the house. "I love you, Poppa!" she shouted as she raced away toward the house.

Moments later she climbed into her old pickup truck and headed down the long driveway. The old farmhouse grew smaller in the rear-view mirror, clouded by the dust her truck was kicking up from the drive. She honestly couldn't remember why she'd hated that old house so much throughout middle school and high school. Most of the kids at school lived in more modern houses made of brick. They also mostly lived with their young, vibrant parents who still worked outside the home and understood about important things like cell phones and the internet and driving a hybrid SUV to take their kids to school. With a sigh, she realized it wasn't that her grandparents didn't *want* her to have what her friends had. They were just older and didn't know much about technology and lots of other things that mattered. They were very frugal and had to know something was justified and practical before investing in it.

She knew she had every reason to be grateful, and was. What it all came down to was that she was already different from the rest of the crowd because of her facial deformity and her stringy, mousy-brown hair. She'd wanted to fit in so badly it hurt, and it didn't help when everyone at school was exchanging text messages and blog pages. She couldn't even begin to count the evenings she'd brushed past her grandparents and raced up the stairs to her room to cry on her pillow. With a deep stab of guilt she recalled how terribly hurt they must have been at the slamming of her bedroom door. They'd only wanted to spend time with her and she'd rejected them time

Donna R Brown

and time again because she was too bitter to accept the comfort that was within arms' length.

Her parents had been killed in a horrible crash when she was only five. She could barely remember the sound of her father's voice or the smell of her mother's lavender lotion, but she would never forget that night. Her parents had driven to Austin that afternoon to hear a favorite band at a downtown club. They were so in touch with their social selves, with the music scene. Nanny had often called them "hippies," and scolded them for "living to the music" and not being more practical.

Ludie had spent the night with Nanny that night because Mommy and Daddy weren't expected to return home until very late. Nanny had tucked her in to the soft bed in the guest room upstairs and kissed her on the forehead. She had just begun to drift off to sleep when she heard Red barking in the driveway, and the crunching of tires on the gravel. She had jumped out of bed and went to the landing in the hallway outside her room and peeked between the slats of the railing to spy. It was Sheriff Dunham and he was looking pretty sad. Brother Joe from the church was with him, and Ludie knew instantly that something was terribly wrong.

She heard Nanny make the most horrible sound, almost a deep, primal wailing, and then watched her back up, wiping her hands feverishly on the dishtowel that had been slung over her shoulder. Nanny was shaking her head fast and saying "*no, no, nooo...*" over and over and Ludie

9

knew. Mommy and Daddy weren't coming back to get her. What would she do? She couldn't live alone back at her house, not without her Mommy and Daddy there to take care of her. Poppa had seen the car coming up the drive from his workshop and had raced back to the house and was just coming up the porch steps when the sheriff delivered the news. He dropped his head to his chest and stood there very silently, not moving for what seemed to Ludie an awfully long time. Finally, he moved to Nanny and pulled her close. She crumbled into his arms and together they'd cried. Ludie ran back to her room, frightened. If Nanny and Poppa weren't okay, she knew she wouldn't be.

Ludie never told anyone she had heard all that. She had just crawled into her bed and sobbed quietly into her pillow and soft quilts for a long time, until she fell asleep. The next morning she pretended not to know anything so she wouldn't be in trouble. Maybe she had dreamed it? When she woke up the next morning there were some members of the church in the living room, and Nanny had led her to the kitchen where Poppa sat over a cup of coffee and sat her down at the table. Nanny had held Ludie's small hands in her own and told her that a man had been drinking alcohol and wasn't driving right. His truck had crossed the line and hit her parents' car. They hadn't even made it to the hospital before Daddy was gone, and Mommy only held on for a few minutes after arriving there.

# Chapter 2

Snapping out of her sad memory, she focused on the farm road she was turning onto to make her way toward town. It was only a few blocks but there were often tractors blocking the flow of traffic and she needed her full attention on the road. Rounding a curve she caught the faintest glimpse of the Blackwater Creek, which ran behind the farm and back around to the highway. The creek, as most everyone called it, was not only a great place to fish, it was also a place of many legends. There were twists and turns that trailed away from the main roads and, for several miles, remained hidden and dark. If not for the sounds of the cars in the distance, it would feel like the edge of nowhere, far from civilization. The expansive pastures were dotted with trees that separated the haunting creek from the rest of the world. Heavy, ancient cypress and cedar trees dipped lazy branches over the dark, murky waters known to be occupied by alligators and water moccasins. Spanish moss hung from low-spirited trees so thick they looked like party streamers hung by melancholy guests at a gathering fit for mourners. The creek had always been a little frightening to Ludie. She'd listened to far too many stories told by nervous little girls on back porches at night.

Blackwater wasn't a big town, as towns go, but it was big enough for Ludie. Aside from the menacing creek bottoms, there were a lot more pleasant features worth boasting. It had the courthouse square with its large, tree-shaded lawn and gazebos close enough for her to eat lunch and spend time reading there most days. The thing about Blackwater was she'd always lived there, and everyone knew her. Most kids had graduated only to get out of there as quickly as possible to start college or an exciting career. Ludie had never been much of anywhere, really. There were times when her former classmates would stop in to eat with their parents when they were home for a weekend away from their busy college lives. Ludie sighed at the thought of it. College and parents. Two more things that everyone else had and she didn't.

Her old classmates had long ago abandoned their bullying tactics, but the sting was still there. Sometimes when they breezed into the cafe she felt like they were judging her for not having moved on with her life. The worst part was that none of them seemed surprised to see her there, as if the expectation had always been that she'd never move on and make anything of herself. *There's Ludie,* they must surely have been thinking. *Still in Blackwater. She never moved on.*

It's not that she didn't think of moving on. But Poppa needed her. He didn't have anyone else, and he was getting on in years. College wasn't her thing, but that didn't mean she didn't have plans for the future. She wasn't going to spend the rest of her life waiting tables, that was for certain. One day she'd pursue her career path and discover her big purpose. One day.

When she arrived at work, the breakfast crowd was assembled, most of them locals who were in their regular seats, telling their usual stories.

"Who needs a warm-up?" Ludie asked, holding up her Bunn pot, ready to pour. The topic of the morning was not, of course, local politics. Blackwater was, for the most part, a well-oiled machine. There were other problems to solve and the men had obviously gotten right to work on them.

"There is no way a damn octopus knows how to predict a good soccer player." grumbled Melvin, no doubt in a grouchy mood in response to what was probably another rejection by his beloved Mavis. "Octopus's don't have brains."

"Then you ought to be able to relate to this one pretty well," snapped Mavis, without missing a beat. Ludie wished she wouldn't be so hard on him. He really was a nice man, maybe a little paunchy in the middle and a bit bald on top, but still a nice man. And he adored Mavis.

"And besides," Mavis continued. It's not *octopus's. It's octopi*," she snapped.

Melvin wiped his bacon-greased fingers on a napkin before nervously adjusting his tie. He had recently forsaken his usual overalls for shirts and ties. He wore a new tie nearly every day nicer than the day before, and all to impress Mavis.

Apparently the news anchors on TV were still talking about the octopus that had been touted as psychic because of his actions that predicted the outcome of the soccer world cup and how he had just recently died.

A few minutes later, Owen walked in and slid into his seat across from Melvin. "I don't want any breakfast today, my sweet tooth's hollering for dessert."

"We've got pie," offered Mavis. "You want chocolate? Cherry? Pecan?"

Before Owen could answer, Melvin retorted, "How about octu-pie?" He looked like his heart would nearly burst in his chest when he saw Mavis crack a smile. *Progress.*

"I don't even know why we're still talking about it," said Mavis, while she busied herself placing silverware on the table. "Soccer is not even a sport that matters much 'round here, and besides, I think it's ridiculous that all those foreigners call it 'football.' Real football," she added with a nod, "is when the Texans play."

The men grunted and nodded in agreement and began placing their orders. No menus were needed as the offerings in the diner hadn't changed as long as Ludie could remember, and the men all had their regulars they rotated as the mood so dictated.

Ludie stepped back to the kitchen and Birdie caught her by the arm. "Sweetie, I need you to pick up a shift tomorrow if you don't mind. I've got Mavis out to a doctor's appointment. I know it's your day off, but I'm gonna' need you."

14

Lucille Odom, or "Birdie," as most of the folks in town called her, had been the owner of the Ladybird Cafe' since it opened twenty years ago. It was a gift from her husband and, when he'd passed away eight years ago, she'd considered retirement but couldn't bring herself to close the cafe.

No one in town would manage it like she would, so it remained in place. Birdie was a tiny little woman with big hair the soft yellow of buttercups. Ludie had never seen her without her blue jeans and big silver belt buckle she'd won as a barrel racer in her younger days. Boots were her shoes. She had no other shoes in her wardrobe. Just about everyone in town loved Birdie, and she loved them, too, although she'd never admit it. She was a tough one, and not prone to emotional displays. Everyone knew how she felt about them, as she was one of the most generous people in Blackwater, although she didn't like a fuss made over any of her kindnesses.

"I don't see any reason why not," Ludie told her, while she loaded a tray with hot plates. "I've got nothing planned for tomorrow."

"That's the problem! You're twenty-one years old and you don't have any plans. If I didn't need you so badly tomorrow I'd insist you go into Houston and find something to do. You need a social life," Birdie lectured, clicking her tongue and shaking her head.

Birdie thought Ludie needed a young man in her life, and told her so often enough to make

Ludie feel self-conscious at the thought of a relationship. Ludie immediately brought her hand to her face, running her fingers across the slight scar on her upper lip. She'd been born with a cleft palate and had corrective surgery as a child, but the scar remained. It was faded with time and hardly noticeable, except to her. She shuddered at the memory of all those tutoring sessions with the speech pathologist. All of that had made her a prime target for school bullies, and she'd never since considered herself a candidate for much of a social life. The scars ran deeper than the surface, although she'd turned out to be a pretty young woman. Her delicate features and pointed chin and nose lent to her air of femininity. People told her she was pretty, but it was usually the older folks in her life like Poppa and Birdie and she'd always thought they were just saying so because they loved her.

In the secret-most places of her heart, she dreamed of a relationship, of a guy to call her own. She often thought of what it would be like to have someone who loved her, who really loved her for who she was. Her daydreams ran deep and often invaded her thoughts at the most inopportune times. She'd be waiting tables and imagine a fairy-tale wedding. She'd be at the library staring past the pages of her book and daring to dream of lying next to the love of her life, whoever he may be. Even the thought of pillow talk and romance made her yearn for more. She'd been embarrassed on more than one occasion when someone would catch her in her reverie and jolt her out of it. It made her wonder if they could read her thoughts and undoubtedly her face was as red as it felt. She wondered if there would ever be someone for her.

The rest of the day passed without further event, although Mavis did take the time to fill her in on Melvin's latest ploy to coerce her into a date. Apparently he'd gotten tickets to the Houston Dynamo game from a former client and needed someone to go with him, triggering the conversation about soccer Ludie had walked into that morning. He wanted to go *ever* so badly, pressuring Mavis more intensely than usual.

"He doesn't have any more interest in soccer than you or me," she asserted. "If it was the Texans playing, I might think about it," she smirked. "He just knows he's getting old and knows he's gonna' need someone to take care of him." Ludie had sighed when she heard this, and felt a bit sorry for poor Melvin. "It won't be me, that's for sure," Mavis told her. "Besides, the game's on Sunday and I have to have some tests run on Monday. The last thing I need is dealing with that man all day right before that."

"Are you okay?" Ludie asked, her brow knit with worry.

"Oh yeah, Sugar, just some routine things that need checkin' out." Her eyes narrowed. "Those doctors will do anything for money these days, you know that."

Later that night back at the farmhouse, she found Poppa sitting on the front porch in his chair, enjoying the night. Ludie walked up the front steps and took her usual seat on the glider swing. She mentioned to Poppa that she was concerned about Mavis. She'd noticed her slowing down a little lately, even gripping the countertops for balance on more than one occasion. Poppa seemed to share her concerns. After a while, Ludie excused herself and went upstairs to get ready for bed. Whatever was going on with Mavis weighed heavily on Ludie's heart, and it was a long time before she finally surrendered to sleep.

As soon as she turned into the courthouse square the next morning, she saw a commotion near the café. A fire-truck and two pickups with a single red light on top of each of the cabs and stickers identifying them as volunteer fire-fighters blocked the street in front of the café. Thick, black smoke curled and rose from the back of the diner. Its contrast was surreal against the blue sky dotted with soft, white clouds. She pulled the truck into a spot in front of the barber shop three doors from the café and ran toward the door. It was propped open with a large hose stretched across the sidewalk and trailing into the café and to the kitchen in back. The good old boys stood vigilance out by the street sign, apparently overcome by smoke. Before she'd even raced through the door she heard Birdie shouting at her younger brother.

"Robert, how many times have I told you that vent hood needs cleaning more often? What were you thinking?" Robert, in his white apron and with a dishtowel slung over his left shoulder was doing his best to explain that he'd kept the vent hoods squeaky clean. Birdie wasn't listening to a word he said in his defense, she just kept right on shouting and running around barking orders and assessing the damage. Dennis, one of the volunteer firemen came bounding through the swinging kitchen door nearly tripping on the hose. A large fan had been placed in the kitchen toward the open back door, helping to alleviate some of the heavy smoke that hung in the air.

"It's okay, Miss Birdie, the fire is out!" Dennis shouted, noticeably short of breath. His department-issued radio was in his left hand and his right hand gestured wildly, pointing to the back in a sweeping motion. "Yep, we were able to respond quickly enough to take her out. You're gonna' have a little smoke damage, of course. Even the big municipal departments would've left you with at *least* some smoke damage." He nodded emphatically. "It couldn't have been completely without damage, even if it would have been handled by the city guys."

After a great deal of commotion and over an hour of constant scurrying about by the firemen, the fire chief, Owen, sauntered in from the back holding a burnt-out junction box up for all to see. "This here's your problem, Birdie. It was singed clear up the cord. We caught it before there was too much damage. You'll have to replace your stove and grill of course, but your bigger ovens in the back and the walk-in cooler look like they've been spared." He looked as though his heavy-duty fire department-issued suspenders would pop from a chest bursting with

19

pride in his men and their quick work. He was known to bristle at the mere suggestion by anyone in town that his volunteer department was any less valuable than a big city department and this would be no exception. Fortunately, everyone knew not to say a word that might damage his fragile ego.

The rest of the day was spent in cleanup. Birdie had called out one of those recovery and cleanup companies out of Houston to come restore her cafe and had been told it would be a few days before they could reopen.

The next morning Ludie woke up much earlier than she'd intended. She'd tried to go back to sleep, relishing a day or two of relaxation, but had given up after a few minutes. This would give her an opportunity to help Poppa out around the house. As she descended the stairs, the smell of fresh-brewed coffee met her in the kitchen doorway. There was a note next to the coffee pot.

*Gone to town to pick up some supplies. Since you're not working today, do something fun. Love, Poppa.*

He'd already left, and had thought to leave her a fresh pot of coffee. Pouring some into her travel mug, she swirled her favorite vanilla creamer into it and replaced the lid. This would be a good day to catch up on some reading. Grabbing her keys, coffee cup in hand, she headed out to her truck.

When she finished at the library by late morning, she noticed a table set up in front of the Blackwater Creek Candle Company. The owner,

Brynn Callaway, was setting up a display of baskets full of potpourri out front and a huge sale sign. Brynn was a friend she'd made during her employment at the Ladybird. She often came in for lunch since her shop was only a few doors down on the courthouse square.

Ludie walked over, shouting a quick greeting to Brynn. "What's cooking today?" she asked, not able to recognize the delectable scent.

"Two things. Gingerbread and Peppermint Stick." It was already halfway through August and everyone on the Texas Gulf Coast was ready to be done with summer. After long, hot and humid summers, most everyone in town looked forward to fall and, as a result, business at the candle shop always picked up when school was ready to start. Even though it was still summer, it was none too soon to start making the autumn scents and, shortly thereafter, the winter favorites.

Ludie stepped inside and breathed in the festive combination of what Brynn had in the melting pots today and what was already stocked in her showroom. It was intoxicating. There were still plenty of year-round favorites like floral scents and aromatherapy fragrances. Elegant displays of spa fragrances lined the walls. Some of the shelves were already decorated in rich hues of pumpkin, chocolate, and gold and only added to the atmosphere. People would be ready for their fall candles almost as much as they'd be ready for the fall weather.

"I heard about the fire," Brynn said, arranging her potpourri and baskets. "How bad is the damage?" Ludie watched her while she worked.

"Not as bad as it could've been. I think Birdie's got some people coming today to give estimates for restoration and repairs." She picked up a lime-scented car freshener and sniffed it, continuing. "Either way, we're gonna' be closed for at least a week or two. At first we thought maybe just a couple of days." She followed Brynn into the work area of the shop.

Within moments of the "open" sign being turned around two ladies came in, taking lids off jars and smelling the candles. Brynn kept a shaker jar near each display that was full of coffee beans. Without thought, Ludie picked one up and gave it a few gentle shakes.

"Here," she offered, handing it to one of the customers. "Smell this between every two or three fragrances. It'll clear your palate. Once you've smelled a few scents, your sense of smell is distorted." The woman accepted it gratefully and the two shoppers continued on their quest for all the right fragrances.

Brynn regarded Ludie with interest and asked, "You really know your candles, don't you?" Ludie had, after all, been a loyal customer since she'd opened the shop.

Brynn's face lit up. "Ludie! That's it! While Birdie's closed, come and work for me! I could really use the help, and I know it's just temporary, but I'll take what I can get."

Ludie perked up at the idea. "Do you mean it? I would love to!"

Shortly after the customers had paid for their candles, Brynn had her in the back teaching her the ropes. After the gingerbread and peppermint stick candles had been poured, they began working on cinnamon and caramel apple. Spice days were just that, she explained, while Ludie listened attentively.

"If you're making cinnamons and caramels and such, you can't just come in and pour magnolia or rain shower. They don't mesh well and the customers don't like it," she told her, stirring a large vat of clear melted wax. "There are separate days for that."

The sensor under the welcome mat chimed, alerting Brynn to a customer. Ludie glanced up to see Mavis, who seemed surprised to see her busily occupied behind the half-wall that divided the showroom from the work area.

"What are you doing back there, working, Sugar? You're not leaving me and Birdie are you?" Mavis asked her, a single brow arched in question.

"Relax, Mavis," Brynn laughed, "I'm not stealing her; I only needed to borrow her for a few days while the diner's under repair." She carried a tray of votives she'd just finished trimming to the front.

"I thought you had an appointment with your doctor, today," Ludie mentioned. "Did you already go?"

Mavis shrugged off the question. "Yep. All done. It was just some routine follow-ups." Ludie wondered what it was she was following up on, trying not to worry. It was no secret that Mavis had seemed more tired than usual as of late, but Mavis dismissed it by mentioning some headaches and saying she'd just had a hard time sleeping lately. After making her selections and paying, she gave Ludie a quick hug. "Now, I'll expect to see *you* back at the diner soon as we open." She threw a playful frown over her shoulder at Brynn and headed out the door.

Ludie ended up spending most of the day placing wick tabs in jars, glancing up occasionally to see Brynn stirring in fragrances and coloring, testing to see that they were just right. Ludie was impressed that she seemed to do it all without recipes, and wondered how the candles always remained so consistent.

"Can I pour some of that into this jar," she asked, holding up a jar she'd just wicked.

"No!" Brynn replied, giggling when she realized she'd answered so emphatically. "This is votive wax, and it's got a much higher melt point. Container wax is softer." She then went on to explain the different grades of wax and their uses. Apparently it made a big difference in the way the candles burned, and if the proper grade wasn't used the results were not good.

Ludie eyed Brynn carefully. She had mastered her craft and Ludie knew it. She moved around her shop like a woman on a mission, her soft, auburn curls bouncing around her face, her mouth pursed in a constant smile of satisfaction.

After Brynn had poured the votives she dispensed some of the softer wax from another melting pot and scented half with sugar cookie and half with black cherry. "They blend well in the shop," she told her. She let Ludie pour her own candle, which delighted her to no end. "You can take it with you," she told her.

Ludie's eyebrows went up as a thought occurred to her. "Can I take it to Birdie? It would really make the diner smell better than all that smoke did."

# Chapter 3

After Ludie worked all day in the shop with Brynn she walked down to the Ladybird Café. She found Birdie talking to a man in a business suit about fire damage and restoration. Both of them looked up when she walked in the room, and Birdie commented on her scent.

"Well don't you just smell like a box of candy," she told her. Ludie smiled, self-conscious over having drawn attention to herself.

"I was helping Brynn make candles," she told her. "It was so much fun!" She jumped back, flustered, when the businessman leaned into her, without warning, and sniffed at her neck.

"Mm...." he moaned. "You smell good enough to eat."

Ludie felt a warm rush that started at her neck and rose up to her face. Her cheeks flushed with color, a reaction that didn't go unnoticed by the man. Ludie excused herself and went to the back of the kitchen before he could further embarrass her. She peeked around the doorway, listening to the conversation.

"My name's Eric," he told Birdie, handing her a card. "Don't forget the name, I can give you the best deal you'll find from someone of professional quality that's willing to come out this far." She took the card, noting the information.

"I'll have to let you know, Mr..." glancing back down at the card, but before she could say his last name he told her she could address him by his first name. "I'm Eric Butler. But to you, I'm Eric."

"We're gonna be friends," he told her, flashing an irresistible white smile. "And friends are on a first-name basis, right, Birdie?" She did not seem impressed, but shook his hand anyway. Ludie continued to watch, unnoticed, from her position in the back. He was a man who was comfortable in his own skin, she could tell. His black hair and coal-black eyes were a perfect complement to his olive complexion. He had gone on to extensively describe his credentials and the important companies he'd done work for in his home town of Chicago. The sheer volume of his contacts had allowed him to build his portfolio and eventually build a business of his own. Eventually he'd relocated to the Houston area in light of the ever-increasing development that was booming along the Gulf Coast. The economy in the Houston area was largely based upon the successful petrochemical industry. The population had the tendency to follow the job opportunities.

Ludie came out from the kitchen as soon as he'd left. "What do you think?" she asked her employer. "Are you going to let him fix the diner?"

"I don't know," she answered, "there was something I didn't really like about him."

"I liked him," Ludie said, before she could stop herself. "I mean, he did seem nice. And very

27

professional." She felt the color rise in her cheeks again when Birdie turned a thoughtful gaze on her.

"Well heavens to Betsy!" Birdie beamed. "I believe our girl's finally noticed a young man," she yelled to Robert who was crossing the dining room towards them.

Ludie was quick to dismiss her accusations, although her facial expressions spoke volumes.

"Um, here," she said, changing the subject before any further humiliation could befall her, "I made you a candle!" Birdie took the lid off and inhaled deeply. It was black cherry, and the wax was a rich, creamy dark red color.

"I love it!" Birdie said, replacing the lid and setting it on the counter. "Sugar, you made this by yourself?" Her eyebrows rose into pointed arches and her smile widened in approval. Robert retrieved a lighter from his pocket and lit the candle.

Ludie glanced at her watch, realizing that most of the day had slipped by. She'd had such a good time in the candle shop she didn't realize how quickly the time had passed. She had just enough time to stop at the grocery store and pick up some things to make dinner for Poppa.

When she arrived at home later in the evening, she noticed Birdie's SUV parked in front of the farmhouse and wondered how she'd beaten her there. She'd only been at the store for a few minutes, it had seemed. Poppa always enjoyed his visits from Birdie. Entering the kitchen through the side door, she found Poppa and Birdie looking through some brochures of appliances and cabinetry and fixtures.

"What's going on?" Ludie asked, picking up one of the brochures.

"Oh, that salesman that came by today was trying to talk me into redecorating the whole diner. I was just showing these to your Poppa to see what he thinks I should go with for the replacement appliances." She had a glossy brochure with photos of industrial stoves and ovens spread out on the table between her and Poppa.

"Oh, you mean Eric," Ludie said, as nonchalantly as possible, turning a brochure over in her hand. She looked back up in time to see Poppa and Birdie exchange an amused glance. They began teasing her about remembering his name, and Ludie did her best to change the subject. Pulling up a chair, she asked, "Well, are you gonna' do it? This is your chance to update the Ladybird! We'll be closed for a couple weeks anyway, this is the perfect opportunity!" She felt herself getting excited at the prospect of a more modern look.

"If you don't mind me sayin' so," Birdie said, "that young man is slick as a catfish. I think he could sell a refrigerator to an Eskimo." Poppa laughed and reminded her that she actually did need to buy a refrigerator as well.

"I went to town this morning," Poppa said, changing the subject. "I happened to see Mavis coming out of the drug store. She didn't see me at

29

first, but I noticed she didn't look quite right. I think you might be on to something, Ludie."

Birdie looked up, her eyes narrowed with concern. "What do you mean, 'not right'? What is Ludie on to?"

"She was walking down the sidewalk, and she started kind of veering to the left," Poppa answered. "If I hadn't come up on her all sudden-like, she'd have stepped off the curb before she knew it." Birdie seemed concerned. She loved her friends like family, and she considered Mavis far more than an employee.

"I noticed it, too, Birdie." Ludie pulled up a chair and sat down. "I already mentioned it to Poppa."

"She said she was fine, just tired," Poppa said. "I'm sure that's all there was to it." He continued sifting through the brochures, commenting on designs he liked and others he didn't feel were as efficient. Poppa had spent many years doing carpentry and remodeling jobs for people in town. He'd long since stopped taking jobs, but his opinion and advice were always valued.

The next day, Ludie woke up eager to get to the candle shop and get started. She was enjoying candle-making, although she tried not to let on too much around Birdie, for fear of hurting her feelings or making her feel like she would leave the café to work at the candle shop. On her way to the shop, she stopped by the diner to ask Birdie what she'd decided to do about the repairs. She hoped Birdie would use this time, as well as the insurance money from the fire claim, to adopt a more modern look. There was nothing wrong with the Ladybird as it was, but it was clearly time for something new. The rust-colored floors were a definite throwback to the 70's, and the red and white tablecloths and matching cafe curtains needed a new look.

She had no sooner entered the diner when Eric walked in behind her. His broad smile made her blush.

"Well if it isn't the sweetest-smelling girl in Texas," he said, causing a blush to rise from her neck to her face. Ludie immediately felt flustered, and struggled for a response. She looked down, licking her lips and drawing in a deep breath.

"I haven't even made any candles yet today," she stammered. "I was just now on my way to the shop." Before she knew what hit her, he reached out and took her by the hand, pulling her toward him. He leaned in to her hair behind her ear, taking a slow, deep breath. His nose tickled her, and made her extremely jumpy. The sensation it caused made her uncomfortable in a pleasant sort of way.

"Doesn't matter," he smiled. "You're already sweet." Ludie backed up, almost tripping over an extension cord that was stretched across the dining room. It was there for the heavy-duty fans that were helping to remove the stench of smoke from the air, and to make Ludie feel even more awkward than usual, no doubt. Eric was a confident, intelligent man, and he even seemed amused at Ludie's discomfort. It seemed to her that he took pride in his power to make her blush. Irritated, she made the excuse that she needed to get to the candle shop because Brynn would be expecting her.

The shop was only separated from the diner by a few shops, but the walk gave her a few minutes to think about what had just occurred. It wasn't that she was embarrassed, really, but she wasn't entirely comfortable with the advances of a man she didn't know. She'd had limited relationships, most notably her best friend in high school, Thomas, but he'd gone away to college and they'd lost touch. Since that time she'd put her focus and attention toward helping Poppa around the house and working. In a town like Blackwater, there weren't many "new guys in town," and she'd known most of the men her age since grade school. Besides, dating just wasn't a priority.

And then this *Eric* had shown up and thrown her off balance. She bristled at the thought. She knew she couldn't take his attention too seriously. He was a salesman. They made their living by being charming. That's all it was, and she'd already dismissed her thoughts of him before she entered the shop.

The day passed quickly in the candle shop, as was typical during such a busy time of year. The Moms found more time for themselves once the children were back in school. The result was a steady stream of customers. It was Ludie's job to take care of the customers in the showroom, but she took every opportunity to learn what she

Donna R Brown

could in the back. Today was an aromatherapy day, meaning Brynn had the melting pots full of herbal scents, such as lavender, patchouli, and other spa-type fragrances. She even allowed Ludie to blend her own batch of a light floral spa scent, which she even got to name once it was finished. It was a soft, aqua-blue color, and it turned out lovely. Brynn agreed that the name "Rainforest" suited the fragrance perfectly.

An aspect of the business she hadn't considered was the wholesale demand from various gift shops and florists. In certain times of the year, Brynn told her, there were fundraisers for schools and youth athletic teams. It was overwhelming at times, and within a few days she'd realized how many times the limited crew stayed late into the night completing orders. There were a few mornings she'd arrived to find Brynn sitting at her desk in the back over a cup of coffee and pharmacology textbook. She'd had to abandon, temporarily of course, her dream of advancing her nursing education during her divorce and was now attempting to challenge some of the courses to complete her degree. It meant hours of studying at her own pace, her only option considering she had a ten-year-old son, Blake, whose father wasn't in the picture. She still had many hours of clinical rotations left to do, which meant she needed to schedule them at times when her son was in school or when her brother, Ben, was able to look after him.

Blake knew he was loved. His mother seemed to fulfill her goals all within his presence, an ideal situation for a single mom. He rode the bus to the shop most days, with the exception of the days his uncle was off work and able to pick him up, and did his homework in Brynn's office. Ludie saw Blake on most days, even when she'd been at the diner, as Brynn often allowed him to go to the Ladybird for a snack after school.

It was a Monday morning when Ludie, Brynn, and a couple of temporary helpers were working frantically on a wholesale order that Eric came into the shop. He was stretching his neck, no doubt to catch a glimpse of Ludie. Why, she'd never understand. He was clearly out of her league and she knew it, prompting her to duck behind a tall stack of boxes. They were packed with twelve large container candles each, surrounded by packing peanuts and waiting to be sealed.

What happened next could've been avoided if she'd had the courage to remain in view and nonchalantly continue her work. Due to her cowardice, though, she'd removed herself from his line of site like a nervous teenager. She never thought he'd actually ask for her by name. She hadn't realized he'd even *known* her name, let alone have the audacity to ask for her. Still, she acknowledged, she was a bit envious of his confidence and ease around people. She'd never have that kind of courage.

When she heard him actually say her name, she became so instantly terrified of even a part of her being visible that she attempted to reposition herself behind the stacks of boxes, knocking a box off the top. Packing peanuts flew in every direction and she saw the jars falling before the glass shattered. She dared to look up and saw a smirk on his face.

"Oh, I, uh..." she bent down and began picking up the jars and placing the jars that could be salvaged on the worktables, and murmured an apology. Brynn didn't seem to be at all upset. On the contrary, she appeared to be rather amused at Ludie's attempts to be smoother. Ludie would deal with Brynn later, she thought wryly. "I was so busy, uh, counting the cases to see how many vanilla creams and gardenias we had. I guess I just lost my balance." She felt the warmth in her face, certain that it must be visible. She was relieved to discover that only one jar had shattered, when she heard Eric's voice again. *His rich, deep voice.* She fumbled with the boxes, dropping more foam peanuts than she managed to put back. Why was she suddenly so clumsy?

"I need to purchase a large candle," she heard him say. Brynn was at the register. "What kind of fragrances do you like? I recommend the pumpkin spice this time of year," she said, opening a jar and waving it beneath his nose.

"I want that one," he said, pointing to the gardenia candle Ludie was cleaning up off the floor.

"Gardenia." Brynn said with a smile. "Let me get you one so you can smell it." She reached toward a display.

"No," he stopped her with a dismissive wave. "I want *that* one." He pointed to the one

Ludie was cleaning up. Brynn's arguments didn't change his mind, and she yielded to his insistence when she realized he was interested in the girl, not the candle.

Brynn smiled when she rang up his purchase, making an excuse to call Ludie to the front. "Can you get me some change from the back, Sweetie?" She smiled at Eric, a grin of conspiracy spreading across her face. It was time for Ludie to have a social life, and if selling a little broken candle every now and then helped, she was more than happy to do her part.

Ludie came to the front with a bank bag full of coin rolls and bills, and handed them to Brynn. Blushing, she offered to get him a gardenia candle, which he declined, whispering, "I've got everything I came for. Thank you, Darlin'." And with that, he sauntered out, empty-handed, with a self-assured grin on his face.

It took Ludie a while to recover, which tickled Brynn to no end. She went to the back and continued cleaning up her mess, careful to sweep up all the tiny shards of glass before anyone got hurt. They spent the rest of the day filling orders, breaking briefly for lunch. Since Birdie was still closed, they picked up hamburgers from a drive-thru and ate in the back of the shop. Brynn's brother, Ben, came in with Blake late in the afternoon. Ben was great about picking up his nephew after school on days he had to stay late for various extra-curricular activities, like soccer practice or tutoring. Ludie had known him back in high school and recalled that he was always very nice to her, even when others had been less than kind. He was a few years ahead of her in age, and had moved away after he'd graduated. He'd come home to take a refinery job in a nearby town and was currently staying at Brynn's, which was a great help to her as he spent a lot of time with Blake.

"Want me to drop these off at the post office?" He asked, pointing to a stack of cases near the door. "Ah, no," Brynn answered, "these go UPS. Do you mind?"

"Hey, Ludie," he said, smiling when he walked past her. "You got anything for me?" He surveyed the cases she was counting.

"No, thanks," she answered, "these are fund-raisers, they'll be picking these up tomorrow." Ben was taller than his sister, but shared the same dimples that were her trademark. Brynn's hair was a rich auburn versus Ben's golden locks, but they both had the same characteristic curls. *Good people*, Ludie thought. The world could use more families like this one, and she smiled at the knowledge that she was considered a friend of the family. It felt good.

"Thanks, Uncle Ben," said Blake, poking his head around the corner from Brynn's office. And, remember, icks-nay on the unk-food jay," he whispered, certain that the secret he shared with his uncle was safe.

"I know pig Latin," laughed Brynn, "and I know you two eat junk food. Just keep it to a minimum." She went outside to help load Ben's car while Ludie continued her work.

Later that evening Ludie arrived at home to find Poppa asleep in his chair. She loved his cozy living room, and smiled at the sight of him. Nanny's chair was still in its spot next to his, and it was as though she might walk in and sit down at any moment. The room was dark, in the same earthy tones from the 70's. Although it was dated, Ludie wouldn't change a thing. It was Nanny and Poppa, and it was home. She leaned over and kissed Poppa on the forehead, clicking off the small lamp next to him. Removing an afghan throw Nanny had crocheted from the couch and covering him with it, she recalled the many, many times she'd watched her grandmother do the very same thing.

She hoped Nanny would be proud of her if she was watching her right now, which she believed she was. Nanny had always wanted her to go to college, but it had never seemed the right fit. She did, however, utilize the strong work ethics Nanny had inspired, a characteristic that had made her so valuable to Birdie and Brynn.

When she climbed the stairs to her room, she felt certain she'd be asleep the moment her head hit the pillow. After a hot shower, she crawled into her unmade, rumpled bed with her still-damp mousy brown hair and her thoughts quickly turned to Eric. Why had he come to the shop? Aside from the broken candle he'd insisted on paying for. And more importantly, why did he ask for her? He clearly wasn't interested in candles since he'd left empty-handed. She turned over and pulled the covers to her chin. She'd have to ask Birdie tomorrow what this guy was all about.

It wasn't very long into the next day before the conversation turned to Eric, even though the next morning when she stopped by the diner there was a heated conversation between Birdie and her brother. Not only did they disagree about the plans for the renovation, but Robert felt as though Birdie had the tendency to put herself into the business of others far too often.

"I'm just concerned," she snapped at him, "and there's no harm in showin' it."

Robert put his hand down on the counter and met his sister's gaze, softer now. "If she wanted you to know, she'd have told you." Apparently the two of them had been discussing Mavis and her possible illness. Mavis, of course, had been rather dismissive of anyone's questions, thanking them for their prayers. Ludie vowed to herself she'd stop by and see her after work that day.

"What's wrong, Birdie? She's still not feeling better?" she asked, crossing the room to where Birdie stood.

"That's just it, child, I don't *know* how she's feeling because she won't talk to me. I've called her twice this week and more than that last week. If she bothers to answer at all she changes the subject." Her expression clearly showed she was troubled.

"I'm sure she's okay, then," Ludie said, hoping to put her mind at ease, trying to sound reassuring, even though she felt a twinge of dread at the thought of their dear friend being ill. "There's probably nothing to tell, maybe she's just enjoying her time off while you fix the cafe."

Bending over to pick up a black trash bag off the floor and opening it to throw away some discarded pieces of sooty sheet-rock, she found her opportunity. "Speaking of the cafe," she drawled, as subtly as she knew how, "what have you decided?"

Robert snorted his opinion of her decisions as he brushed past them both to take some trash outside. He stopped to take the one from Ludie's hand and whispered, "You'll be sorry you asked." She laughed dismissively as he walked outside.

"Well? Did that Eric guy talk you into making some changes?"

"I don't know," Birdie answered, thoughtfully. "Robert seems to think I need to gut the whole place and start from scratch. I'm a bit more sentimental and don't want to change too much." She looked down at her fingernails, picking at a cuticle. "Besides," she smiled sadly, "my late husband gave me this diner, and we fixed it up together."

Ludie took a seat on the barstool next to her and wrapped an arm around her shoulder. "Birdie," she whispered, "it's good that you have those memories. But change is good, too. He'd be proud of you, I mean, if he could see what you've done with the place."

Birdie laughed sarcastically. "Yeah, he'd love the soot. Nice touch."

Ludie shook her head. "You know what I

mean. You've built a strong business here, with a devoted clientele. Our "good ole' boys club" is lost right now. Ben and Blake saw them all over at the Dairy Queen after school. Who knows where they're going for breakfast these days?"

"I don't know, Ludie. Maybe it *is* time for a change." Her face lit up with an idea. "Will you help me? I mean, will you help me choose the designs? I don't know a thing about decorating."

Ludie squealed her delight. "Do you mean it? I would absolutely love to!" She jumped to her feet and rushed over to the windows, gesturing grandly. "I can see it now! New window treatments, and the tables... the tables, we can go a little more modern, but still keep the diner look."

Birdie shook her head. "What have I started?" she moaned, not fooling Ludie with her worried expression. She could tell Birdie was almost as excited as she was. Almost.

Her excitement left her as quickly as it had come when Eric came to mind. Since he'd had the lowest bids, he'd already been selected to do the job. He had presented Birdie with a very professional-looking proposal, complete with glossy photos and computer-generated before and after shots. Knowing that Birdie wasn't completely sold on the full renovations, he'd thought ahead and provided the specs on both the basic bare minimum repairs as well as a full, grand-scale renovation. Birdie, of course, had to admit both to him and to Ludie that she'd liked what she'd seen.

Eric came back that evening and he, Ludie

and Birdie spent some time at one of the booths that hadn't been damaged poring over brochures and paint samples. On more than one occasion Ludie glanced up and caught Eric looking at her. Again, she felt the color in her face. Why did he have that effect on her? And on that note, why did he seem to enjoy it so much? She did her best to focus on the photos he was showing them

"Oh," breathed Ludie, "I love this one. Birdie, look." She'd selected some dark cherry wood tones that would add some sophistication, yet not take away from the diner atmosphere. There were some laminate floors that were much lighter yet blended well with the color-scheme. He recommended custom tile work over laminate though, since a café would have a much higher volume of traffic than a home. She was impressed with the selections he'd brought, convinced that he was very good at what he did.

Before the end of the evening, Birdie had made some concrete decisions on the dining room, but reserved opinion as of yet on some of the appliances. Robert, after all, was the one who'd be using them the most, and she wanted him to have some say. She told Ludie as much, and then asserted, "It's not like he gets the final word, of course. He needs to remember his place." Anyone who knew Birdie knew that she loved her brother more than she let on; her efforts to convince anyone otherwise didn't work.

Ludie glanced up, meeting Eric's gaze, and smiled when he winked at her. Maybe he wasn't such a bad guy. Maybe, she admitted to herself, she'd gotten the wrong impression. She'd never been very comfortable with male attention, but that was certainly no fault of his. She'd take a page from Birdie's book and reserve judgment until she had more information.

It's not that Eric bothered her, really. It's just that his gaze was so intense. His eyes, black as onyx, bore into her and she could feel the heat deep in her chest. His rich, dark hair and his perfect complexion set her slightly on edge. It wasn't just that a man was noticing her; it was that such a truly magnificent man was noticing her. Even his scent was intoxicating, making her subconsciously lean into him while she was gazing across to look at the images on his laptop screen. *It's just cologne, Ludie,* she thought. *Any man can buy cologne, that doesn't make him any better than other men.*

# Chapter 4

The next afternoon Ludie was at the candle shop alone, doing some cleaning up. She managed to get a few jars wicked and a few votives wrapped, but she wasn't yet confident enough to pour candles on her own. She'd wait until Ben got back with Blake before she started getting too adventurous and creative. Ben didn't exactly refer to himself as a candle maker, but he did know the basics. He'd helped out on more than one occasion when they had deadlines. She didn't want to get too far ahead of herself, but Thanksgiving was coming up in just a few weeks and Brynn was busy doing some clinical rotations. Her semester was nearing its end within a month and then she would have to complete a minimum number of clinical hours. The theory portion of her nursing program was self-paced, but her clinical hours had to be scheduled according to the availability of nurse preceptors. Brynn would need as much help as she could get in the coming months.

The phone in the shop rang, and Ludie answered. "May I help you?"

"It's me," Brynn said. "I'm at my clinical shift. Will you do me a favor?"

"Sure, whatcha' need?" she asked her, moving some jars to a different workspace.

"I'm over here at the cancer center, in the

back. I'm learning to manage central lines in the chemo room. The girls up here want to see the candles. Will you bring me a case of jars, I don't know, maybe all the fall scents? That'll give them some choices." Ludie started looking for an empty box to fill while she listened. "Oh, and some votives, if you can manage carrying them all," Brynn continued. "It's a lot to carry. If you'll call my cell when you drive up, I'll come out to your truck and help carry them. I've just got to be careful not to draw too much attention while the big bosses are still here. They should mostly be cleared out of here by the time you get here."

"Want me to close the shop?" Ludie asked her.

"Nope, Ben should be there shortly, and he won't mind watching the shop. Thanks, doll!" They hung up, and Ludie began gathering the appropriate candles and packing them in boxes.

Just as Brynn had told her, Ben and Blake arrived shortly after, and Ludie already had her boxes loaded and ready. Ben helped her out to the truck with them and she left for the hospital.

A few moments later, when she followed Brynn into the clinic, they chatted while they made their way down the halls toward the treatment center. When they rounded the corner to the chemotherapy rooms, her heart dropped in her chest at what she saw. Sitting in one of the lab chairs, with her sleeve rolled up to expose an IV line with two small ports, was Mavis.

Ludie rushed over to her, horrified. "Mavis! What's wrong? Why didn't you say anything?"

Ludie captured her in an embrace, and then pulled back to look her in the eyes.

"I didn't want to get anybody all worked up," Mavis sniffed. "Not until there was anything for sure enough to tell." Ludie looked her up and down, focusing on the line in her arm. "I would think this is for sure, at this point!"

Mavis looked into Ludie's tear-filled eyes. "I know, honey, I know. But you and Robert and Birdie have so much to deal with right now, what with the diner, not to mention you helping Brynn out with the candles."

*Brynn*. Ludie felt a brief wave of anger rising and turned back to look at Brynn, who stood helplessly watching the conversation unfold. "How long have you known?" she asked her, realizing that she wasn't at liberty to share the information with anyone due to all the privacy rules. Ludie didn't know who to be angrier with, Brynn or Mavis, for keeping this secret.

"You know I'm not allowed to talk about it," Brynn pleaded with her. "It's the privacy act. Besides, I knew you'd have to come in to bring the candles, and..." she trailed off.

The realization that she'd intended her to find Mavis this evening struck, and she apologized. She knew Brynn couldn't say anything, especially with Mavis telling her not to. She was lucky Mavis wasn't angry with her for having Ludie bring the candles now. "I'm sorry, Brynn. I know you had to do what was right." Leaning in to hug her, she whispered in her friend's ear, "Thank you."

Fighting tears, Ludie turned her attention back to Mavis. "Well, what matters is, I know *now*, and we can get through this together." She sat down next to her and held her hand, leaning close to enable them to talk quietly. "Mavis, how bad is it? What are the doctors saying?"

Mavis elaborated on the results of her tests with Ludie. Apparently it had all started with dizziness.

"They said I had an "altered gait," whatever that means. It got worse over time and then I started getting pretty bad headaches."

She'd not wanted to trouble anyone with her problems and had kept it to herself. Once Ludie had informed her that kind of secretiveness wasn't acceptable within their circle of friends, she assured her that they would all get through it together.

"Ludie," she said, forcing an uncertain smile, "If you don't mind, let's not worry Birdie with this yet. I'd appreciate it if you didn't mention it to her quite yet."

"As a matter of fact, I *do* mind," Ludie said, assertively. "Either you tell her or I will. Partly because I don't want you to go through this alone, but mostly because I know she'll kill me for not letting on."

Ludie made sure it was okay with Brynn that she let Ben stay and close the shop so she could stay with Mavis until her chemo session was finished. The two of them discussed the severity of her brain tumor and how they would manage. When Mavis's infusion finished dripping, a nurse came and disconnected the line and flushed it with two syringes of liquid. She helped Mavis get to her feet and gave her some brief instructions to follow in the event of side effects. When they left the clinic, they went by Birdie's house in town and told her of the situation. Birdie cried and hugged her, and the three of them vowed to fight it all the way. Birdie didn't seem to be too surprised. Ludie knew she'd considered all the possibilities and braced herself for the worst.

The next day on the way to the candle shop, Ludie stopped by the diner to talk to Birdie. Eric was there again, supervising a crew that was installing some flooring. Ludie was impressed, and told him so.

When she called Birdie to the side to talk, she kept noticing Eric was looking at her from across the room. One of the things that gave Ludie the most comfort was the knowledge that Birdie had taken out some policies for cancer and long-term care for herself and Robert and Mavis some time back. "We're not getting any younger," she had told her at the time.

When they'd talked a few moments, Ludie surprised herself by having the nerve to approach Eric and ask him about the renovations. He offered to sit down with her over dinner and discuss the plans.

"Um," she said nervously, "isn't that something you should be discussing with Birdie?" fully aware of his motives for asking her, yet still a bit excited at the prospect.

"Absolutely," he said, flashing a gorgeous

smile. "I don't make a move in the diner without Birdie's okay. But I do know how much she values your opinion, and there are a couple of extras I want to surprise her with. You may be the only one who knows her tastes well enough to know how she will react."

That evening after she helped Brynn close the shop she raced home to shower and decide what to wear. Poppa couldn't help but notice something was different when she came downstairs, her hair down and styled with soft curls framing her face instead of the usual ponytail. She licked her lips, touching the scar on her upper lip self-consciously, wondering if Eric had noticed it. If he had, he hadn't seemed to mind, and she had a warm feeling in her stomach at the thought of him.

She saw a smile beneath Poppa's moustache and began defending herself before he could even ask. "It's just a business dinner, Poppa. We're going over renovations for the Ladybird."

"So you and Birdie are meeting him for dinner."

"No. Birdie's over at Mavis's tonight," she said. She was quickly becoming defensive. "I agreed to meet him instead." She looked at the floor, tucking loose tendrils of hair behind her ear.

"What's going on with Mavis, anyway?" Poppa asked. After taking some time to explain about her tumor and the planned course of treatment, he mentioned that he would like to be there for Birdie while she helped Mavis.

"She's got more than enough on her plate as it is, dealing with the restaurant and all. I should go over tomorrow and help her out, and make sure she doesn't need any help with Mavis." Birdie and Nanny had been friends for many years, and Ludie thought it was very kind of Poppa to be concerned.

Glancing up at the clock, Ludie said, "I need to get going, Poppa." She gave him a quick kiss on the forehead and raced out the door.

She and Eric had agreed to meet at the Ladybird, and when she drove up, she saw him, standing next to his sleek black sports car. *How very appropriate*, she thought. *Of course. What else would he drive*? She parked and got out, nervous in her steps, convinced if she didn't take her eyes off him she would trip over the curb. His words rushed through her like hot blood coursing through her veins, making each step less certain.

"C'mon, Sweetheart, you look good enough to eat and I'm starving." He held the door open and she lowered herself into his car. She was very impressed, and he knew it. They agreed upon Mexican food. A few minutes later he got onto the freeway. They had some time to chat on the way into Houston. Before she knew it, they were being seated at "Amigos," a trendy, upscale restaurant in the Rice University area.

He ordered two margaritas on the rocks, despite her insistence that she didn't drink. "You need to live a little, relax," he murmured, looking into her eyes.

She took offense; she was certain he was

accusing her of being uptight. *I am not uptight,* she convinced herself, studying hard at the menu to avoid the intensity of his gaze. The waitress returned with their margaritas, and they placed their orders. She took a long sip to show him she would. He smiled as if he knew that.

"So," she began in a small voice, "what are your plans for the diner?"

Looking into her eyes he told her without wavering, "I don't want to talk about the diner."

"That's why we're here," she reminded him.

"No," he said, "we're here because I couldn't stop thinking about you." He seemed so very aware of her discomfort, and what's more, he seemed to thrive on it. Instead of angering her, it only served to flatter her.

They talked into the night. After sipping her way through two margaritas and enjoying a wonderful dinner, she felt herself becoming much more relaxed. She didn't expect to become so comfortable with him. The alcohol warmed her veins, and Eric warmed her heart. He had taken her by surprise, and she felt herself giving in to the emotion. His intensity became far less threatening when she realized how genuine his interest in her seemed to be. It was a feeling she wasn't accustomed to, yet she already found herself craving it more and more.

When their dishes had been cleared away and she'd finished her second drink, she realized how late it had gotten. She reminded Eric she had to work in the morning and should get home, and he agreed, mentioning he had some clients to meet with before going to Birdie's in the morning.

The drive back to Blackwater was nice. She felt much more relaxed with Eric than she had on the way to dinner. Soft music played in the background while they talked. The moon was full, and a thick layer of fog danced above the ground. After they'd crossed the Trinity River bridge, she realized he didn't take the turn she thought he would. When she asked him about it, he said he wanted a little more time with her and it was worth taking the scenic route.

She failed to suppress a chill when she realized they were going to drive right through the woods and across Blackwater Creek. The moon shone through the clouds and cast a blue light on the pastures below. Branches from cypress trees hung heavily on the ground beneath them and exposed a sad, eerie glow. The thick blankets of fog played tricks on the eye, and Ludie was sure she detected movement beyond the wind in the trees. The hair on the back of her neck stood up and she shivered, hugging herself closely and rubbing her arms to keep warm.

Eric didn't fail to notice and offered his jacket.

"I'm not cold," she whispered. "I'm just… I'm all right."

"No, you're not all right. I just saw you shivering. What's wrong? Talk to me," he commanded, gently but firmly. Oddly enough, it made her feel more secure.

"I just never liked being near the creek. Too many ghost stories when I was a little girl.

Too many rumors and stories of things happening down here."

"You're safe with me," he murmured, his hand stretching across to rest on the back of her neck protectively. She felt herself relax and savored the warmth and comfort of being with someone so protective of her.

When they arrived back in town, Eric asked her how she felt and if she was okay to drive. She assured him she was fine after all this time and that the margaritas had had little effect on her. He pulled up in front of the Ladybird and walked her to her truck.

She was surprised, but relieved, when he didn't try to kiss her. She was so unfamiliar with the dating world, and wasn't sure how she would have reacted. He told her good night and reminded her to drive safely, then got back into his car.

She felt intoxicated, but not by the drinks. His masculine scent, his deep voice, and good looks combined, creating a far more dangerous drug than alcohol. She hadn't expected to feel this way, and wasn't sure what to do with that. It was exciting, she had to admit, but it was unnerving as well. The interest he showed in her was flattering. After all, she was a small-town girl, and he was a bit more on the sophisticated side. He didn't seem to have any of the confidence issues that plagued her, and he had certainly already made his mark on the world, judging by the sleek, sexy car that probably cost more than ten times what her truck had when it was new. The rich leather interior and high end briefcase, smart-phone, and other technology that seemed to be always at his fingertips spoke of financial accomplishment.

As she drove home, she cracked the windows of her truck open slightly and relished the warm glow she felt. Every song on the radio spoke to her on some level. Was it supposed to feel this way? She wondered. Her mind drifted for a moment to the café but snapped immediately back to Eric and how he'd made her feel. She gave some thought to Mavis's condition and her concerns, and again, Eric took her thoughts captive once again. Determined to focus on the candles just to keep from letting her hopes of having a relationship take control, she continued her drive home. She'd briefly noticed headlights in her rearview mirror but quickly dismissed them. As she turned onto the farm road, however, she realized it was Eric, and she saw him turn around, flashing his lights at her to let her know. *He followed me home!* she thought, again feeling the warm comfort of his attentions flowing throughout her body.

The lights were on in the house, but this time Poppa wasn't asleep in his chair. He was on the porch, waiting for her. She felt a twinge of guilt for not calling, but before she could apologize he just stood up, huffed, and said "Good night," then he turned and entered the house.

"G'night, Poppa," she breathed, ashamed of herself; she bit her lip nervously when he disappeared ahead of her. She raced up the stairs and to her room, breathless with excitement

Donna R Brown

as she threw herself onto her bed and opened her diary. It was unsettling, feeling two very different emotions at once. Her excitement about Eric and her guilt about Poppa battled for her attention.

The next morning her first waking thought was of Eric. She hadn't dreamt of him that she could recall, but knowing he was on her mind when she fell asleep, she wouldn't be surprised if she had. All she knew was that her day-time dreaming was of him, and if she could remember the dreams of her sleep, she was sure they would be as well. Glancing at her clock, she calculated how much time she had before she needed to start getting ready for work.

Knowing she could afford a few more luxurious moments in her soft, comfy bed, she snuggled down into the covers and relished the extra time.

Once she had gotten up and showered, she was ready to start her day. When she went downstairs she found Poppa at the kitchen sink, rinsing out the coffee pot. His mood seemed to have improved slightly.

"Are you hungry?" he asked her, offering her a muffin. She took it and removed some butter from the refrigerator.

"Thanks. What do you have planned for today?" she asked, knowing he was dressed to go out, which merely meant he was wearing one of his nicer sets of coveralls. He had worn those things for as long as she could remember, but there were definitely separate ones designated for working around the farmhouse and others for

55

going out.

"I'm going to see Birdie and talk to her about what we can do for Mavis." For the first time she noticed the toll his concern was taking on him. Cancer brought back painful memories, and he'd actually become quite experienced in being a caregiver during Nanny's struggle. It didn't surprise Ludie that he wanted to help out where he could.

She ate her cranberry muffin and then swept the crumbs into a pile and off the edge of the table into her hand. "I'm going to help Brynn today," she offered. "She stays so busy this time of year." Giving him a quick kiss goodbye, she followed him outside and got into her truck.

Upon arriving at the candle shop, she noticed there were already a couple of customers milling about looking in the window at the displays. She was happy for her friend, knowing the income from this shop was not only helping her raise her son but financing her education.

They spent the morning wrapping votives and making gift baskets. She learned that even with as many walk-in customers as they had, the bulk of her business came from wholesale and mail order. She also learned that although the candles were the most obvious and popular items, there was a large demand for her fragranced soaps, lotions and air fresheners as well.

Shortly before lunch one of Brynn's regular customers came in, carrying a partially burnt candle. Roxanne was a feisty redhead, and her

Australian accent was unmistakable.

"I just can't smell this one," she was telling Brynn. "It needs to be stronger." Brynn guaranteed all her candles, and was notorious for doing re-pours on a whole batch based on the smallest of complaints from a single customer. She got few complaints, however, because of her attention to detail. Roxy, as she was known, was a breed of her own, though, and was very specific about what she liked and didn't like. The candle she was returning was *Red, Red Rose*, and her complaint was that it wasn't strong enough.

"Couldn't you just add a bit of oil to it, like you've done before, Luv?"

When Brynn explained to her that with a fragrance like the roses, the oils are very heavy and can extinguish the flame.

"Ah, I'll make it work," she told her. "I don't care what it looks like when it burns, I just want the bloody scent." Brynn took the candle and told her she'd work it over and to check back in a couple of days. Ludie was amazed at this woman's unmitigated gall. *She'd make it work? She just wanted the bloody scent?* Her confidence was a bit over the top, as far as Ludie was concerned. Brynn knew what she was talking about when it came to candles, and Roxy just wasn't getting the message. *If a candle won't stay lit, you can't very well "make it work" now can you?* Ludie thought.

She watched Roxy as she browsed the shop, going through all the displays, removing lids and smelling the coffee beans in between. She tended to annoy Brynn with her particular demands, but she was a good customer so they did what was needed to keep her happy.

Roxy had a very worldly and sophisticated air about her. She was apparently quite successful in the lingerie business somehow, although Ludie wasn't certain to what extent. There didn't seem to be a huge demand for high-end lingerie in a town like Blackwater, so perhaps she also sold it online. Roxy had traveled the world, something Ludie envied because she'd not had the opportunity to do so herself. She was beautiful, and carried herself like a Hollywood starlet. Everything was coordinated, from head to toe. The lipstick matched the nails, and both matched whatever she wore on any given day. This was a woman who took care of herself and it showed. Ludie wished she could be more like that. She rarely had the nerve to apply more than a soft pink lipstick and seldom wore eye makeup. As for blush, she didn't need it because she blushed naturally almost any time someone looked her way. As she continued the mental comparison between herself and Roxy she realized what she felt wasn't annoyance but perhaps jealousy. Ah, what she wouldn't give to be a woman so clearly in control of herself.

Unbidden, her thoughts turned to Eric again. She wasn't used to being scrutinized so carefully. Eric studied her every time he was near her, and always managed to leave her on edge. She didn't know if that was a good thing or a bad thing.

Roxy's comment brought her out of her reverie. "What's on your mind, Luv?" Ludie giggled at her accent.

"Nothing, just these candles," she answered quickly, glancing back up at her.

"Ah, you can't fool me, Luv, you were dreaming about a bloke," she said, surprising her with a wink. I know a girl with a man on her mind when I see one."

Ludie smiled at her. "Yeah, I guess I do, a little bit." She smiled, waiting for nature's makeup to color her cheeks. "Are *you* seeing anyone, Roxy?"

The redhead looked up with a conspiratorial smile. "Ah, a few here and there. Not settling out for any one man just now."

"All right, then. That makes sense. Me too." She smiled at her white lie. "I supposed I do have a 'bloke' on my mind. I had dinner with him last night. It was the exception for me rather than the rule," she confessed. "I was a nervous wreck. I don't go out much."

Roxy flashed the smile of a woman on a mission. "Ah, Darling, you just need to learn to be more comfortable in your own skin. Stick with me a while and you'll get there." The brash redhead was quickly growing on her.

Roxy put her purchases on the counter and began digging in her purse. Here, give me your number and I'll put it in my phone. You come out shopping and spend a day with me and you'll get the hang of it. No need in being afraid of people when you can take a page from my book and make *them* afraid of *you*."

Ludie gave her the number, and asked for hers as well. There was something about Roxy she really liked. Perhaps she had misjudged her. She wished more than almost anything she could be more like her. Bold, sassy, and confident, yet with the kind of personality that put people at ease. Eventually.

After work she drove over to Mavis's house to check on her. She didn't answer the door until after the third knock, which concerned Ludie. She knew Mavis could hear her knocking because her little Chihuahua, Bitsy, was yapping excitedly from the time she stepped onto the porch. When Mavis finally came to the door she seemed weaker already. The treatments were taking their toll, even though they had only just recently begun. Mavis gave her a hug and asked her to sit down, pointing to a rocking chair with a soft cushion directly across from hers. Her little house was charming, and Ludie had always loved to visit her.

"Can I get you something to drink?" Mavis offered.

"Oh, no, thanks. I just stopped by to see how you're feeling." She glanced down at her hands in her lap, and looking up, asked her if she'd told any of her family what was going on.

"You and Birdie and the others *are* my family," she told her. "I have a nephew in Houston but he's busy. He got married recently and is finishing up his bachelor's degree. I don't want to bother him with all this."

Ludie met her gaze fully then. "Mavis, I

know he wouldn't consider this a burden. I remember how happy he was when you made it to his wedding."

Mavis smiled at that memory. "He does mean a lot to me, and my staying in touch with him would've meant so much to my sister." Mavis had lost her sister to breast cancer a year before, and had worked to stay in contact with her nephew ever since. "I'll call him. I will. I just want to see how things progress with the treatments first." She went on to explain that bringing up the subject of her diagnosis would be sure to upset her nephew with a new set of worries after losing his mother to a completely different type of cancer.

They talked for a few moments about her treatment plan, and then Ludie shared with her some of the plans for the diner. Mavis gave her opinions on some of the options, although she tended to be more like Birdie in that she liked things the way they were. "If it ain't broke, don't fix it," she'd heard her say many times.

Ludie helped her by doing a few quick chores, and then explained she needed to get home and see about Poppa's dinner. She reminded Mavis to call her if she needed anything, and she assured her she would. It was painful to see her struggling so much, and Ludie vowed to herself to help her fight her way through this battle. Mavis had always taken such good care of her little house, with a place for everything. Ludie had always enjoyed visiting her, and Mavis in turn, had loved it when she came by.

The next day Ludie arrived at the shop for her shift to find Brynn surrounded by cases of supplies that had just arrived. She was pulling things out as quickly as she could, with the excitement of a child.

"We got all the new Christmas scents!" she shouted. "Come smell!"

Ludie joined her, removing the lids and breathing in the fragrances. Stopping long enough to retrieve a couple of shakers of coffee beans to sniff between scents, she raced to the front. As soon as she rounded the corner, she found herself face to face with Eric, surprised she hadn't heard the chime when he'd entered. Brynn had Christmas music blaring. The melodic sounds from Kenny G's saxophone really lent a festive atmosphere to the shop.

"What are you doing here?" she asked him before she could stop herself.

"Well thanks for making me feel so welcome," he laughed, apparently unaffected by her rudeness.

"I didn't mean it like that," she giggled, "I was just surprised to see you. I thought you'd be out on a job today."

He cleared his throat. "I was. I had to make a trip to meet with my cabinet guy and got back into town earlier than I expected." He leaned over and kissed her on the cheek. The beginnings of a warm smile were interrupted by a cough. "It's just the smells," he explained, covering his mouth. "I just wanted to let you know I had a great time last night, Amigo."

She smiled at the reference to the restaurant where they'd eaten. She told him to stop by anytime. "I had a great time, too."

He told her he was needed down at Birdie's, as apparently she'd consulted with Robert on the appliances and had made some decisions. He would probably spend most of the afternoon there working up some prices and time frames on his laptop. He encouraged her to stop by when she had a break, that he'd love to see her, and then left for Birdie's.

"So what's the story?" Brynn asked her when she returned to the back with the coffee bean shakers. It was obvious she'd been eavesdropping because the volume of the music had been conveniently turned down shortly after he'd arrived. "I knew you'd been talking to him about the renovations, but didn't realize you two were going out." She lifted a brow in curiosity, clearly expecting all the juicy details. Ludie hated to disappoint her with the fact that there *were* no juicy details. Not yet, anyway.

Waving an open bottle of winter pine oil under Ludie's nose, she asked her, "Isn't this divine?" It wasn't Ludie's favorite, but she didn't want to hurt her feelings. She did open a bottle of spiced cranberry that she loved. There were oils of peppermint, egg nog, pumpkin spice, bayberry, hot cocoa, apple cider, and many others. They both turned up their noses at a sample of roasted chestnut the company had included. It smelled more like roasted road kill, they decided, giggling amongst themselves. It was about that time that

Ben came in through the front with Blake following closely behind.

"What's up? Ben asked. "Didn't anyone ever tell you two to stay away from inhalants?" he asked dryly, looking down at them and all the bottles of oil surrounding them. The two were clearly delirious, either from exhaustion after all the extra hours they'd put in or from the heavy scents of the oils.

Blake looked up from his hand-held game. "Thanks, Uncle Ben."

"No problem. Go do your homework and stay away from these two. Remember, buddy, just say no." He laughed, looking over his shoulder as he walked out the door. "Have fun, ladies!"

After work that day Ludie headed straight for the Ladybird. *To check on the status of the renovations,* she told herself. When she saw Eric's car in front of the diner, she couldn't help but smile.

She found Eric and Birdie at the corner near the windows going over some plans. They were gorgeous, Ludie admitted to herself. He was a very creative man, and had clearly been blessed with talent. She could hardly wait to see the finished product.

Birdie offered her some iced tea, which she happily accepted, and brought up the subject of Mavis.

"She told me you went by to see her yesterday evening," Birdie smiled. "You know, that meant the world to her. She went on about it, but I think she was also trying to keep me away from the subject of her prognosis." Her eyes were filled with worry and Ludie could tell this was taking a toll on her.

"You love her so much, don't you Birdie?" At this, Birdie snorted in an attempt to sound un-phased. "Well of course I *care*, I'm gonna' need all my employees when we re-open, you know." She wasn't fooling anyone, and she knew it. Ludie knew she was one of the most caring, compassionate people she'd ever met and that being part of Birdie's inner circle meant she was like family and there was nothing she wouldn't do for her little family. Her tough exterior rarely tricked anyone, yet she kept it up doggedly.

Ludie surprised her with a quick kiss on the cheek as she got up to take her glass to the kitchen. "Stop that," Birdie ordered, and tried to suppress a smile.

Ludie found Eric in the kitchen, discussing particulars with Robert who, as it turned out, was more than opinionated about how things needed to be arranged around *his* stoves, and *his* workspace. Birdie had finally given up and yielded control of the kitchen to him, which pleased him to no end. He seemed most excited about the wrought-iron rack Eric was going to have installed over the workspace for his pots and pans.

When she walked in, Eric looked up and flashed the most incredible smile she'd ever seen. She wasn't sure why this man had such an effect on her, but she'd pretty much abandoned herself to it, anxious to see where it would go.

"I'll be finishing up here shortly. Want to go

for coffee?" He looked up at Ludie expectantly.

"Sure. But I can't stay out too long, Brynn just got in a ton of supplies and we're going to get an early start tomorrow."

# Chapter 5

Over the course of the next two weeks, Ludie and Eric were inseparable. She was overwhelmed by his attention and it felt nice. He'd invited her over for dinner at his place twice, and she was surprised he was such a wonderful cook. She offered to help him in the kitchen the first time, but he'd dismissed her with a wave of the hand, saying "I've got it. Let me take care of you this time."

As he began to prepare, she was glad she wasn't helping. He seemed to have a wonderful knowledge of fancier foods, as opposed to her more down-home, country style of cooking. She didn't know what a shallot was until he'd told her. To her it looked like a mal-formed onion and she wouldn't have really known how to use it in a dish. He opened up a world of gourmet to her and she liked it. The richness of the sauce, the aromas from the kitchen, and the wine that was perfectly suited to the meal impressed her and he seemed to know it.

On one occasion he mentioned to her that he wanted to meet her grandfather. She decided there was no time better than the present, and he followed her home that very evening.

Poppa was in his "stay-at-home" coveralls,

and she wished she'd called ahead to warn him. He didn't seem to mind, though, and appeared to be completely at ease in Eric's presence. Ludie couldn't help but feel a bit uncomfortable, though, since Eric seemed to be used to far more sophisticated surroundings than Poppa's humble abode. She wouldn't change a thing though, since the farmhouse seemed so embodied with Nanny's tastes and her loving touches.

The meeting was going well, over all, and she was glad she'd finally introduced the two of them. She was caught off guard when Poppa asked Eric exactly what his intentions were with his granddaughter. She felt butterflies in the pit of her stomach when he looked Poppa in the eyes and told him, "I intend to make her mine. I intend to make her the happiest woman in the world." He looked over at her with a smile, and Ludie wished the moment would last forever.

Until, of course, Poppa answered curtly. "Just see that you do." Poppa had no hesitance at all when he looked him dead in the eye and said, "She's all I got. She gets hurt, somebody else is gonna' get hurt." Poppa tried to look threatening but he couldn't disguise the protective feelings he had for her.

Ludie felt her eyes fill with tears. Not only had this beautiful man just expressed his intentions to make her his, but her beloved grandfather had made it clear how much she meant to him. It was the best day she could remember, and she found herself wondering what Nanny would say if she were still alive. She hoped

Donna R Brown

that she would approve and be proud of her.

Ludie walked him out to his car, and he took her in his arms. "You know I meant every word of that, don't you?" She looked up at him and smiled, almost afraid to answer.

"I feel the same way, it's just that..." she trailed off, unsure of how to express what she was feeling.

"That you don't want to get your hopes up," he finished for her, making it clear he knew her well enough to echo her thoughts. "I'll not disappoint you," he murmured into her ear, drawing her closer.

She pulled away and looked into his eyes. "I believe you, and I trust you."

Thanksgiving was drawing near, with only a few days to prepare. The plan was to have dinner at the farm, and include Birdie, Robert, Mavis, and Eric. Everyone was planning to bring something, except Mavis, of course, because they'd informed her they had it covered. She did not need to try to stand up in the kitchen and prepare anything, they told her. Birdie more than made up for it by writing her own name next to most of the side dishes on their preparation sign-up list. Robert was making the turkey, and Ludie and Poppa were going to bake a ham.

Eric had agreed to bring dessert and showed up with a cranberry orange tart and a pumpkin cheesecake. They were both divine, and Ludie wondered aloud if he'd missed his calling.

He looked up at her sharply, and snapped, "Maybe you should reserve judgment until you see the finished product of my work."

Ludie felt her face grow warm as she realized he thought she was criticizing his work as a contractor. "I didn't mean..." she stammered.

"Forget it." He attempted to soften his stare. "You didn't know any better."

Throughout the rest of dinner Eric seemed more distant, quieter. She was clearing away the dishes after everyone had left when Poppa walked up behind her. "What was that about?" he asked. "Seems to me your city boy is a little on the sensitive side."

"Poppa, it's okay, really. I think he was just a little nervous being around all of us together for the first time." She felt slightly sickened having to make excuses for him. "Besides, I shouldn't have insulted his work."

Poppa didn't seem appeased by that excuse, and his expression remained firm. It would take a while, Ludie realized, for him to get to know Eric and understand him better.

The next day Eric took her Christmas shopping in Houston. He didn't bring up the incident from yesterday and she didn't either. She was surprised Brynn had given her the day off, since it would be a very busy shopping day. Ben and Blake had signed on to help her, so she said they'd be fine and encouraged her to go shopping with Eric.

They went to The Galleria, one of the nicest malls in Houston, and she selected a few gifts. For Birdie she got a wall hanging set that would accent the wall near the kitchen in the diner. It would match her new décor beautifully, and she could hardly wait to give it to her. For Mavis she got a beautiful soft knit hat and some silky pajamas. In the past few weeks she'd already begun to lose her hair and now had some purple radiation markings on her head. The hat would be perfect for keeping her head warm and matched the soft pink of the pajamas. For Brynn she bought a beautiful blown glass aromatherapy oil burner for her house. She didn't dare buy any fragrances to go with it, knowing Brynn would have everything she wanted to go with it at the shop. She also got her a new Littman stethoscope she'd heard her mention. She would need it while she finished her nursing degree and even beyond that when she'd be hired as a nurse rather than a student on rotations.

Spotting a game shop, she grabbed Eric by the hand and pulled him in that direction. "Blake!" she said. "I can't forget Blake!" He helped her sort through the selections of games but, since neither of them knew what kind of system he had, they ultimately decided it would be best for her to give him a gift card so he could select what he wanted. When she suggested getting something for Ben, he snapped, "I didn't know he was on your list." He shrugged it off when she pressed him to explain, but even then she noticed his mouth in a set line, his jaw clenched. She sensed his under-riding anger and shrank back from him.

As they continued shopping, his mood seemed to grow mellow. She convinced herself she had over-reacted.

For Poppa, she bought a study Bible reference, knowing that he usually spent the last few moments of his evenings reading his Bible, rifting through the pages to find certain verses before falling asleep in his chair. She loved that his Bible was so well used, the soft leather cover noticeably worn.

When they finished shopping they decided to have dinner at a restaurant near the mall. There were so many great choices, but Eric ended up choosing one he was familiar with, and Ludie was very pleased with his choice. Even though he'd moved to Houston from Chicago only a couple of years before, he seemed as knowledgeable about the city as anyone she knew. They shared some Thai lettuce wraps and another appetizer and finished with the most decadent cheesecake she'd ever had. She carefully avoided any reference to the cheesecake he'd made for Thanksgiving, but he eventually brought it up.

"It's better than mine, that's for sure," he told her.

"Oh, no," she assured him. Yours is the best I've ever tasted, I promise!"

His dark look seemed to reveal his discomfort and he quickly changed the subject. In time, his mood seemed to lighten. After they'd finished eating, he suggested she stay with him that night.

"It's late, and your grandfather is probably already sleeping," he reasoned. "Besides, you're supposed to get an early start at the candle shop to make up for today." He was speaking of casual, every-day events, but his eyes told the real story. His steady gaze bore into her in silent expectation.

"I'll need to go by the farmhouse and get some clothes and things, and I can leave a note for Poppa." She blushed at the thought of staying with him, but had known it would eventually happen.

A couple of hours later she had gathered a few necessities and left Poppa a quick note saying that she was spending the night in town so she and Brynn could get up early and get started at the shop. She was uncomfortable with the idea that she was lying but Eric reassured her that she wasn't stating any untruths. She knew that her letter intentionally gave the impression she'd be staying at Brynn's, but she kept it as it was and left with Eric.

Later, she looked around his apartment. It was a renovated upstairs loft facing the square opposite the courthouse, which obstructed Birdie's café from its view. As always, Ludie loved his apartment. It was as modern and high-end as he was. There was so much white, she thought. Gray, red and black accents finished the look. She was amazed at how thoroughly modern and well-decorated it was, and she told him so.

"It's what I do," he told her. "Remember? It's my calling, although some may not seem to think so."

"Eric," she breathed, "I'm so sorry, I told you I didn't mean it that way... I was..." He put his

73

fingers over her mouth, cutting her off.

"It's all right," he whispered. "I'm over it."

She showered and changed, and went back into the living room, brushing the waves of her chestnut hair as she walked. He looked up from a book he was reading and she felt herself blushing under the intensity of his stare.

"Turn around," he told her, patting the leather ottoman in front of him. He took the brush from her hand and began brushing her hair with long, gentle strokes. When he had finished, she moved from the stool to the couch next to him.

He opened his arms to her as she sat down, and she laid her head on his chest. In spite of her exhaustion, they talked late into the night. When it was time to go to bed, he sensed her fears and her hesitance and whispered words of reassurance to her. When she finally lay down with him, she was sure of their relationship, and sure that she was ready for this next level. An undeniable magnetism was building between them, and she couldn't deny it. Her head fit perfectly in the hollow between his shoulder and neck. For a long while he simply held her. She settled into his embrace, no longer wanting to hold back. She gave in to him, and was shocked at her eager response to his touch. Her tension melted away, and she wasn't nearly as overwhelmed and nervous as she thought she would be. Later, she drifted off to sleep, secure in his arms.

When she opened her eyes the next morning and looked at the clock next to his bed, she surprisingly had no regrets. She was glad she'd stayed with him, and felt even more so when he woke up and pulled her closer to him.

She told him twice she needed to start getting ready for work before he finally released his hold on her. He wanted her there with him, and she knew it. An hour later, they'd had coffee and she was dressed and ready to leave. His apartment was upstairs from a law firm across from the courthouse, so she only had a few steps to walk to get to the candle shop.

When she arrived, Brynn was already hard at work, and singing along to the radio. She seemed in an unusually good mood, in spite of the complete state of chaos the shop was in. The shelves in the front had been perused, and several of the displays were bare. All the melting pots were on at full speed, and Brynn was already pouring. She glanced up when Ludie walked in.

"Black Friday was *incredible!*" she announced. "We sold more than twice what I had hoped. Now we have hardly any candles, and the place is an absolute mess!" Joy bubbled in her laugh. She was clearly pleased with their success.

"Where do you want me to start?" Ludie asked her.

"Straighten up the displays out front and make a list of what we need most. I have 280 pounds of unscented wax already melted, ready to go."

Ludie started arranging the displays, noting the scents that were needed the most as she went. She rearranged some of the displays to make them look fuller, then went to the back and assembled a few baskets of coordinated gifts, matching candles, soaps and air fresheners together to fill in the spaces on the shelves. When she gave Brynn her list, she began transferring jars she'd previously wicked to the pouring tables for her. The wicking rods were already in place in dozens of metal votive molds, and it wasn't long before the scents of Christmas were in the air.

"So tell me," Brynn said, "how was shopping yesterday?" Her raised eyebrow and dimpled smirk told Ludie she knew she'd spent the night with Eric.

"It was great. I got most of my shopping done, even though I haven't bought Eric's present yet. I don't have a clue what to get him."

"That's not the kind of details I wanted," Brynn said. "How was it?"

"What do you mean, 'how was it'?" Ludie blushed, before breaking into a huge smile. "It was *fantastic*!" The two of them were laughing when Ben and Blake walked in.

"What was fantastic?" Ben asked.

"Oh, nothing," answered Ludie, and grasped for anything she could think of to change the subject. "I heard y'all made a killing this weekend."

"Yes, we did!" Blake answered for Ben. "We had people lined up all the way to the door! I helped wrap candles and put them in bags for people," he stated proudly. I earned my PlayStation 3, didn't I, Mom?"

"You worked pretty hard," she told him, "but that's between you and Santa."

Blake rolled his eyes and murmured, "Whatever," Ludie and Ben shared an amused glance.

In the early afternoon a delivery came from the florist. It was a dozen red roses, and had a card signed in Eric's writing.

*To a wonderful night, and to many, many more. Love, Eric.*

She held the card close to her chest as she leaned in to smell the roses, and was surprised to be able to detect their delicate scent in the midst of so many other fragrances that surrounded her. She would take them home later, where she'd be able to enjoy them even more.

Ludie and Ben worked the finishing tables together, where the jar candles were heat-processed and the wicks were trimmed. She took great pride in seeing the smooth, creamy texture and rich colors of the container candles as she cleaned the jars. Her hands were aching by noon, however, from all the wiping, wrapping, and trimming they'd done.

There was a steady stream of customers throughout the morning, and they took turns out in front taking care of them. By noon they'd managed to do a pretty good job of replenishing the shelves but hadn't even begun to fill orders. That would mean working extra all next week to get them completed, but Ludie didn't mind. She loved every minute of it.

Brynn still had several clinical hours to

complete toward her degree and would be in the emergency room two evenings next week, leaving Ludie and Ben to work on wholesale orders. They would be busy, she knew, but they could do it.

# Chapter 6

When Tuesday arrived, Ludie and Ben were working hard. Eric arrived to find the two of them working fast and furious, laughing over a shared joke. In spite of the complete innocence of the moment, Eric was clearly offended.

She looked up and smiled and walked over quickly to say hello. As she approached him, she felt him grow tense and his expression seemed cold and distant. Overcome by a cough, he moved away from her.

"Eric, what's wrong?" she asked, upset at his reaction. "I've been thinking of you today," she whispered playfully in an attempt to improve his mood. It didn't work.

"Yes, clearly you were thinking of *me*," he snapped. "I could see that."

"Eric, we're working. That's it," she whispered, embarrassed at the thought of Ben overhearing their conversation. She glanced over and noticed he didn't seem to be looking up from his work. He was amazingly tactful, and she appreciated him for that quality.

"Fine," Eric answered flatly. "I need to get going. I just dropped by to let you know I had some proposals to make today. I've got a huge house that took some flood damage a while back. It'll probably keep me tied up most of the day.

Hopefully they won't be burning any candles over there, I need my inhaler as it is just from being here."

She gave him a quick kiss on the cheek, but noticed his response was cool. She returned to the workroom when he left, and Ben looked up without saying a word.

"I'm sorry you had to witness that," she said.

"None of my business," he said, putting his hands up. He gave her a half smile and turned back to his work.

"No, really. It shouldn't have happened, and I'm sorry."

They continued their work into the afternoon and the subject never came up again. Her thoughts kept returning to Eric, until finally she texted him to ask how his bids were coming along. He answered quickly, and apologized for his behavior earlier. She was relieved to have that behind them, and made it a point to not let anything happen again that would make him uncomfortable.

The two of them stayed busy, along with Blake's help. He'd come out of the back room, bored with his games and eager to help.

The door chimed and a woman came to the front. It was Roxy or, as they referred to her in the shop, "Red Rose," after her complaints about the red rose candles. It came as no surprise when she handed Ludie a red rose candle and told her it wouldn't stay lit. Brynn had tried to tell her the last time that if she added fragrance the weight of the oils would extinguish the wick, but she hadn't listened.

Ludie surprised herself at the burst of attitude that came forth. "What happened to 'I'll make it work, I just want the bloody scent?'"

Roxy tilted her head back, then narrowed her eyes and glared silently at Ludie for several painful seconds that seemed more like minutes. Ludie drew in a sharp breath. She wasn't backing down.

Suddenly, Roxy threw her head back and laughed. "That's more like it, Luv. There you go with that attitude, *that*'ll get you through." She gave her a wink. "That's what I like to see!"

Ludie liked her more and more with time, and wondered if she could become as worldly and sophisticated as this gust of wind from down under. With the proper tutoring, she predicted she would.

Ben kept himself busy in the back, pretending to ignore the two women as they laughed and talked. Glancing over at him, Roxy asked, "Who's the handsome bloke?" She didn't even attempt to keep him from hearing.

"That's Ben," Ludie answered, "Brynn's brother. He's helping her out while she's doing her clinical rotations for nursing school."

"Well, hello, Ben," she drawled in a honey-sweet voice. "Such a darling bloke you are to help your sister like this."

That evening Ludie went home tired and aching. She appreciated the satisfaction of a job well done, knowing that Brynn would be pleased with the number of candles she and Ben had made.

She was a little disappointed when Eric hadn't called by bedtime. She debated calling him, but finally decided he might be tired from the clients he'd spent so much time on. Poppa had gone to bed early, and the house was quiet, so at a little after ten she went upstairs to get ready for bed. The clothes she'd been wearing smelled of cinnamon, cloves, and apples, and she was ready to feel clean. She showered and put on her favorite pajamas. Her last thoughts before drifting off to sleep were of Eric.

When she hadn't heard from him the next morning she called. The call went straight to voice mail and she told herself again he must be busy with his clients.

She had other things on her mind this morning, and attempted to dismiss her concerns about him. Birdie had called yesterday and told her that Mavis wasn't doing well. She told Ludie she had made some soup to take by and that Mavis had only been able to take a few small tastes of it before she'd become nauseated again. It broke Ludie's heart to hear how her dear friend was suffering, and she decided to stop by for another visit.

When Mavis answered the door, Ludie could see how weak she was already becoming. It was hard to imagine that only a month or two ago she'd been keeping up with Ludie in the number of tables she was able to juggle at a time at the Ladybird. Ludie offered to do a few chores, but apparently Birdie had taken care of most everything yesterday. Mavis's house was always charming, but now there were undeniable signs of her condition. Her coffee table and kitchen counter were littered with various medical supplies and prescriptions.

She sat down next to Mavis and chatted with her for a while. After a short while, she couldn't help but notice how tired her friend was getting. She helped her to her bed and lingered for a few minutes after tucking her in, holding her hand and looking into her eyes.

"You know you can beat this," she whispered. Mavis smiled weakly and told her she would be fine either way. Her radiation and chemotherapy series were completed and now she was waiting to get some scans done to determine if there had been any growth or shrinkage since the previous scans.

Ludie told her she'd lock up on her way out, and gave her a kiss on the cheek. When she got into her truck, she fought back tears. *Of all the people who could've been struck by this,* she thought, *why Mavis? Gentle, loving Mavis.*

The day at the candle shop passed quickly. When they finished their orders for the day and closed the shop, she still hadn't heard from Eric. Trying to get her mind off him, she agreed to have dinner with Roxy.

They drove in Roxy's red Jeep to the boardwalk in Kemah. "I'm tired of the little country dives in Blackwater," Roxy said, unapologetically. "Besides, we need to go where you can have a little drink and knock off some of that stress."

They ended up spending several hours out, having drinks and lingering over appetizers, then strolling around the boardwalk. Roxy missed the nights in the city back in Queensland, she told Ludie. She loved the lights and the energy that always seemed to somehow evolve from relaxing evenings. As they walked about, peeking in and out of shops along the boardwalk, she spoke of her home.

"Back in Queensland, we do things differently, right down to the way we spend an evening."

"How so?" Ludie asked, and was genuinely interested. She had never traveled much.

"Well for one thing," Roxy answered, "we take our bloody time. Here, everyone's in such a *hurry*. Hurry and get to the restaurant, hurry up and seat us, hostess. Hurry and take our orders. The appetizers should have already been here." Ludie giggled at her friend's honest assessment of American diners.

"In Australia, we take our time. Whether it's a night at home or dinner out, we relax. Appetizers and drinks shouldn't be rushed. We might spend a good long time having a little wine and talking. What's everyone's bloody hurry here, anyway?" True to Roxy's word, they made it a slow and relaxing evening.

The next day Ludie went straight to the Ladybird when she parked her truck. She wanted to see the progress and find out when Birdie anticipated being able to reopen. At least, that's what she told herself was the reason. When she walked in, the first thing that caught her eye was the dark, rich wood tones. In spite of it being all booths and no tables, the new look seemed more sophisticated and somehow classier than before. She took in the changes with appreciation.

The countertops at the register and front counter were topped with beautiful gray-colored granite marbled with the accent colors Birdie had chosen. Ludie would have never thought of blues and greens for a diner, but was pleasantly surprised at the cooler atmosphere they provided. Birdie's paintings and antique-looking country-kitchen décor had all been damaged in the fire, so everything was new. She was pleased to note that Eric had found a way to integrate Birdie's love of Texas nature photography. The blues and greens of the fields of bluebonnets in some of the paintings brought out the colors of the granite surfaces. She would never have been able to visualize the concept, but had a deep appreciation for the finished product.

She found herself looking around for Eric, but he was nowhere to be seen. Birdie came out from the kitchen drying her hands on her apron.

"What do you think?" she asked, gesturing grandly across the dining room.

"I love it!" Ludie cried, turning around slowly to take it all in. "When are we opening again?"

Birdie laughed, waving off her question. "Don't get too excited. This is all that's done. We're still waiting for Robert's stove and grill.

They had to be custom ordered and Eric said it'll be at least another week. Plus they have all the flooring to do in the kitchen, and the brickwork and backsplashes over the stove."

"Still," Ludie said, peeking through the opening above the counter, "so far it's fabulous!" She craned her neck, hoping to see the master of all this creation.

"If you're looking for Eric," Birdie said, "he's not here. He had a job to do and was making a run to Houston. He said he'll be back later to do some measurements for the bar and he's narrowing down some price quotes."

Standing near the front window a few moments later, Ludie craned her neck to look across the square to the street that ran from the opposite corner for Eric's car in front of his apartment. She decided to busy herself and grabbed a broom that was propped against a wall.

"I've never seen so much dust in all my life," snapped Birdie. "This whole thing is turning out to be a major headache. Although I do have to admit your young man has done a good job."

*My* young man, she sniffed. It would be nice to know for sure.

Ludie glanced up to see Eric's car parking in front of the diner and she put the broom back where she'd gotten it. Eager to see him, she ran her fingers through her hair and brushed off the front of her blouse as she walked toward the door to greet him.

She was shocked to see a beautiful woman in the passenger seat, her head thrown back in laughter. Eric seemed to share her buoyant mood. Walking around to open her door, he smiled broadly, happier than she'd seen him in a while. Together they walked up to the door and entered.

He seemed surprised to see Ludie there, but quickly recovered and introduced the woman.

"This is Katherine. She's renovating a beautiful home on some acreage outside of town and we've been in Houston all morning looking at samples."

The woman eyed Ludie with interest. Eric went on to explain that Katherine was one of the most sought-after socialites in Houston. Organizations lined up to put her name on their events and fundraisers. It struck Ludie as odd that Katherine didn't seem to react with any humility at all. It was as if she thrived on being told how elite she was.

*She certainly looks the part*, Ludie thought, and struggled to hide her discomfort. Everything about her spoke of fabulous wealth.

"Actually," purred Katherine, taking off her leather gloves and holding them neatly in her hand, "I'm taking a break from that. My husband's abroad on business so I've got the ranch house to myself for a few months. I intend on making it mine. In every sense of the word" she added, turning a suggestive smile to Eric. She placed one elegantly manicured hand on his chest possessively and the other on his shoulder. Her silky voice added to her appeal, and her mouth curved into a seductive smile.

Ludie felt uncomfortable with the entire situation, and excused herself to the counter to pour herself some coffee. Birdie looked up from the back and flashed her a sympathetic smile. As she swirled some creamer into her steaming coffee, Eric approached her.

"What's wrong?" he asked.

*As if you don't know,* thought Ludie, but disguised her repulsion with a neutral stare. "Nothing," she answered. "You do seem to be a bit cozy with your new client, though." She regretted it the moment she said it.

"Ah, that," he replied. "To borrow your line, we *were* just working." With that, he turned and walked toward Katherine who was waiting rather impatiently near the front door.

Ludie was furious and didn't bother to hide it. Birdie continued her clean-up work in the back and mercifully didn't press her for answers. Ludie retrieved the broom and began sweeping furiously, her knuckles white from gripping the broom handle so tightly as she swiftly stroked back and forth, back and forth.

"I would hate to be a dust bunny right now," Birdie remarked.

After Eric drove Katherine home, he thought of Ludie as he drove back into town toward his loft. He smiled in amusement at Ludie's earlier reaction to the woman. It wasn't as if he'd never had two women interested in him at the same time. *Still*, he thought, *it wasn't bad to experience it again.* It only served to remind him of his effect on women. He found Ludie entertaining in her wholesome naiveté. She amused him, for now. The bottom line: she was his for whatever he wanted to do with her. Katherine however, intrigued him. She was a woman of means, of power, and he intended to experience both qualities firsthand.

That evening Ludie stopped by the candle shop to find out when she was needed to work again. She wrote down the hours Brynn had told her and took a few moments to note the new inventory that was now amply filling the displays. She complimented her on it, and the two chatted for a while.

When Ludie later walked out into the cool night air, Eric was standing near a street lamp waiting for her. He smiled, sheepishly, and approached her with a kiss.

"I was insensitive," he told her. "I was upset with you for being so friendly with the candle boy and I responded inappropriately. Katherine is a client, nothing more. I'm sorry if we made you uncomfortable."

*We,* Ludie thought, and then chided herself for being so petty. She took Eric's outstretched hand and walked with him down the sidewalk to his apartment above the legal firm.

Once inside, the two sat and talked, taking the opportunity to discuss recent events. He was apologetic, and clearly he seemed to be upset with himself. They talked late into the night, and she almost fell asleep after she'd curled up in his lap.

She told him she had an early day with

Brynn the next morning and that she had better head back to the farmhouse.

"Pretty soon I'm going to fix that," he said, gazing into her eyes.

"Fix what?" she asked, sitting up.

"You. Having to leave at night. I don't like it." He murmured, nuzzling her neck. "And I'm going to fix it." She was too shocked at his suggestion to offer any objection. She took in a deep breath, her heart pounding in her chest. He didn't bring up the subject again right away, and she was glad. It wasn't a topic she was ready to discuss. She hadn't seen it coming and needed time to absorb the idea.

After a while, he walked her to her truck and kissed her goodnight. As she drove home, her thoughts kept returning to him. She felt a warm sensation deep in the pit of her stomach when she thought of his place being her home. As much as she loved Poppa, they both knew the time would come when she would leave the nest for good. *And this just might be it,* she told herself.

# Chapter 7

Early in the morning she got a call from Birdie. She was calling from the hospital.

"It's Mavis," she told her, breathless with nervous excitement. "She kept getting weaker, bless her heart, and we took her to the emergency room. Robert drove us, and I sat in the back seat with her. She can't keep a thing on her stomach, bless her heart. All I knew to do was just to hold her until we got here."

"Slow down," Ludie told her. "Where is she now?"

"I'm sorry, honey, I'm just a little worked up. She's here, at the hospital. They wanted to keep her. They said something about her 'white count' being too low and that she could get infection. They make me wear a mask when I go into her room. I tried to tell them cancer's not contagious but they said it was to keep *Mavis* from getting sick." Birdie sucked in a deep breath and continued. "They call it reverse isolation since it's to protect her and not the visitors." If the situation hadn't been so serious, Ludie would've had to laugh at Birdie, knowing she must be giving the nurses a fit.

Ludie hung up the phone and immediately began dressing and gathering her purse and keys. She would give Brynn a call and let her know she'd be late this morning. Brynn would understand. She was the type to be compassionate as always and her reaction confirmed it. She told Ludie to take as much time as she needed and to make sure Mavis was all right before coming to the shop.

When she arrived at the hospital, she found Mavis's room and saw a bright yellow metal cart outside the door. A sign on the door read, "See nurse before entering."

She quickly located the nurse to make sure it was okay to enter. The nurse explained the isolation process and went on to say Mavis was very weak right now and needed to stay in the hospital long enough to build up her strength.

Moments later, Ludie entered the room, masked and gowned according to the nurse's instructions. She wasn't at all surprised to see Melvin in a chair next to the bed, a worried frown on his face.

"I just heard," Ludie said. "I'm sorry I didn't get here sooner."

"Sugar, I'm okay," Mavis told her, through thin lips that were pale and dry. "They're just being extra careful with me, that's all." It was so like Mavis to reassure everyone around her, in spite of the fact that she was the one in danger.

Melvin sat dutifully by her side, looking at her with an expression of love that touched Ludie to her core. *Everyone should be loved like that*, she thought.

As she sat next to Mavis's bed, her thoughts immediately turned to Eric, and she found herself briefly wondering if he would be the one who would love her that way. She had barely had time to think of his request that she move in with him, and she mulled it over in her mind now. Poppa would be disappointed in her, and tell her it's not right to live with someone without benefit of marriage. He would tell her if she was good enough to live with a man and pick up his dirty socks, she was good enough to carry his last name.

Things were different now, though, and Poppa would have to realize that. With so many marriages ending in divorce these days, maybe it wasn't such a bad idea to live with someone first, to make sure the compatibility was there.

She stood next to Mavis and offered her ice chips from a Styrofoam cup. Mavis slept most of the day, so Ludie tried to keep the room as dark and quiet as possible. Melvin made a trip to the cafeteria and to the gift shop and returned with a cup of coffee and a newspaper. He had a very hard time sitting still and when he finished reading the paper he was up pacing in the room. Late in the afternoon he convinced Ludie it was all right for her to leave, since Mavis was resting well.

When she left the hospital she headed straight for Birdie's to let her know Melvin was with Mavis and that she seemed to be resting okay since Birdie had seen her that morning. As she pulled up in front of the café, she saw Eric walking out with Katherine. *Again.* The two of them were laughing about some shared joke, no doubt.

Ludie slammed the door of her truck when she got out, drawing Eric's attention. He smiled and walked toward her, while Katherine waited on the sidewalk.

"Hello, Amigo. Where have you been all day?" he asked.

"I was with Mavis. She's really sick."

"I'm sorry to hear that, really I am," he said, turning to look back at Katherine and then back to Ludie. "I, uh, I'm sorry, babe, but we were just heading out to meet with the electrical guys at her place. They're probably already there, as a matter of fact." He smiled apologetically and gave her a quick hug, joining Katherine back on the sidewalk. Katherine eyed them with an amused lack of concern. To the contrary, she maintained an air of confidence and satisfaction.

Ludie waved goodbye to Eric and entered the café to talk to Birdie. It finally occurred to her to wonder why he had been leisurely walking along with Katherine, laughing over some joke, if they were so late to meet with the electrical guys. And why were they suddenly in such a hurry now?

The rest of the day Ludie had a vague, dismal feeling that she attributed to her concerns about Mavis. Even after talking with Birdie and arriving at the candle shop to help Brynn, she couldn't seem to shake it. It wasn't until the next day after she'd spent more time with Eric that her concerns eased up.

By the end of the week she and Eric had

discussed her possible move at length, and she made her decision. She was not looking forward to telling Poppa. When she finally did, he reacted exactly as she had suspected he would, but she couldn't have prepared for the look of disappointment in his eyes.

She busied herself with packing, assuring Poppa she wasn't gone out of his life forever; she would still be out at the farmhouse often. She would even spend the night there when Eric was busy on jobs. It hadn't seemed to appease him, however, and he still seemed to be a bit uncomfortable around her, as if it took a great deal of restraint to keep from telling her how he really felt.

The tension of the previous weeks finally diminished with the busy-ness of the plans for her to move in. She thrived on the excitement that came with being part of a couple. She couldn't have predicted the joy she would feel at the prospect of picking out a few items for the apartment.

By the end of the weekend, she'd transferred most of her clothes and personal items to Eric's and had placed most everything in the closet and drawer spaces he cleared out for her. Her first night to come home to his apartment from work, she arrived to find fresh flowers on the table, with a note that read *Welcome home. Love, Eric.* She read the card and pressed it to her chest, warm with the excitement of her new and budding relationship.

That excitement hit a road-bump, however,

when Eric had gotten home from work one evening to discover the bed unmade. She had laughed it off, telling him she didn't see the point in making a bed if the plan was to just crawl right back into it at the end of the day. He had furiously ignored her, going into the bedroom and making the bed with neat hospital corners and arranging the pillows in perfect order.

When it started getting late, he showered and dressed for bed. With his hair still damp, he walked straight from the bathroom, pulled back the freshly made covers, and climbed into bed. She hadn't known whether to laugh or cry until she saw the intensity of his anger. He'd made his point, and she never made the same mistake again. Every morning since, their bed had been neatly made. She had excused his display of emotion, realizing that everyone had their own quirks and that she would need to be considerate of his.

One day while Eric was working, she brought home a fresh pine tree in the back of her truck, and immediately set out to decorate it. She struggled to pull it up the stairs by herself, tempted as she was to wait for Eric. It would be worth all the effort just to be able to surprise him. She'd purchased blue and silver ornaments and beads and after finishing the final touches on the tree, she lit some lovely Christmas candles she'd placed on the coffee table and on the bar. Suddenly remembering Eric's asthma, she quickly extinguished them with a wave of disappointment. Standing back to survey her handiwork, she glanced at the clock, eager to see his reaction. When he came home that night, he hugged her and thanked her for making it feel like home. That warmed her and made her realize that it *had* begun to feel more like a home.

One night during her third week in the apartment, Eric didn't come home. She had gotten home from work late, expecting him to be waiting for an explanation, only to find the apartment empty. She looked for a note, but there was none. She stripped out of her wax-stained work clothes and took a long, hot shower, then dressed in a soft nightgown. She climbed into bed, too tired to even read, and then found herself unable to sleep. She had checked her phone for texts, and finally her phone rang shortly after midnight.

"Hey, Amigo," he breathed, "you okay?"

She sat straight up in bed, relieved to hear from him yet disturbed at his casual attitude. "Yea," she whispered, "just worried about you."

"Don't worry, I'm fine. I came to Houston to meet with some tile vendors and ended up staying late to have drinks. By the time we got outta' there I figured it was too late to drive back, so I got a room."

"I've been sitting here worried about you and you're out having drinks?" she demanded. "Thanks. Thanks for letting me know something," she finished with a hint of sarcasm.

"Babe, I'm sorry, really. I thought we were just going to discuss the plans over dinner, then we had a couple of drinks, and I didn't realize how much time had passed."

"Whatever." She was in no mood to be placated.

"I can come home now. I just need to check out of my room and then probably have some strong coffee. You know how much I hate to drive after having more than a couple of drinks."

Feeling guilty, she said, "No, I don't want you taking any risks."

"I'll be home early, tomorrow. I promise. I'll stop by and see you at work."

"Mm, okay," she said. "Get some sleep." Relieved that he'd made the choice not to drive after having drinks, she pushed aside her frustration with him and wished him a good night.

# Chapter 8

By the time the weekend rolled around again, Ludie was excited to have a couple of days off. Ben would be helping his sister in the shop, which meant Blake would also be on hand to help out. She knew Eric was working Saturday, so she spent some time with Mavis then went out to the farm to visit with Poppa. He was still a bit reserved around her, and his obvious disappointment left an ache in her chest.

Sunday, however, Eric was not working and the two of them had planned to spend the day in the museum district. It was meant to be a relaxing day, so she'd pulled her hair back in a simple ponytail and had forgone makeup. When they walked down the stairs and stepped outside, he turned and looked at her, frowning.

He was looking directly at the scar on her upper lip, and she felt her cheeks blazing under his scrutiny. "You forgot to put makeup on," he told her. "I'll wait."

She felt her face burning hot with embarrassment, and hurt. She realized with a flash of pain that he either didn't want to be seen with her or couldn't bear to look at her without her camouflaging her scar.

"Never mind," she snapped. "We don't have to go." She fought back the tears that threatened to spill over her lashes but lost the battle. Turning away from him, she raced up the stairs and bolted back into the apartment. She heard him stomping up the stairs behind her and, when she threw her purse down, she heard him slam the door.

"Do *not* dismiss me," he ordered, grabbing her upper arm and spinning her around to face him. She started to speak, but was silenced by his dark, angry glare.

"When I offer to take you somewhere, you need to show some gratitude. Just remember, you had your chance. I'll be at Katherine's. I need to get some things done out there, anyway." With that, he turned and walked away, slamming the door again behind him.

After she heard his car start, she threw herself across the bed, sobbing into her pillow. She rubbed her upper arm where he grabbed her, realizing his fingers had dug into her skin with his nails. Examining her arm, she saw bruises already forming. Another rush of tears caught her off guard, and it occurred to her to question her options.

It wasn't easy seeing him with Katherine so often. She knew that the woman's country home was palatial and undergoing a complete renovation. According to what Eric had told her, they had gutted the home one room at a time and were creating a masterpiece. It was a very lucrative contract for Eric, and she knew it meant a great deal of money for the job. Ludie knew in her heart there was more to their friendly behavior, but every time she asked him his mood had grown dark and defensive. It wasn't worth it to her to question it.

She could feel her heart breaking in her chest, surprised that it was an actual physical pain that threatened to cripple her. She was puzzled by his abrupt change of mood, and terrified at his violent outbursts. She'd been so excited about starting her life with him. Her friends and co-workers had heard no end of her excitement. She'd spoken so openly about her new beginning and how wonderful it was that Eric had chosen her. She, the one with the cleft lip scar and the mousy-brown hair, had dismissed their warnings: that it was all happening too quickly and she'd rushed in anyway; now she was paying the price. She couldn't exactly go back and tell everyone they were right and that she'd acted prematurely. No. That would be too humiliating and she couldn't bring herself to do it. Besides, she loved him. She would simply have to have an earnest talk with him and resolve their issues.

Communication was the answer. He would have to be more respectful of her feelings and she'd have to take more pride in her appearance. Relationships were about compromise, and she was willing to do whatever it took to make it work. She was perfectly willing to meet him halfway, but she would not accept his blatant disregard for her feelings. Or his embarrassing behavior, flaunting his far too comfortable relationship with one of his female clients. She laughed bitterly, thinking it would have been nice if he'd given Birdie and her café half the time and attention he'd given Katherine.

Christmas passed quickly with everyone focusing so hard on the renovations at Birdie's and filling all the orders at the candle shop. Ludie had begun dividing her time between the two, and had little time to dwell on her worries. Mavis had made some improvement and, upon her discharge from the hospital, had finally accepted Melvin's help. He spent most of his days at her house, looking after her. With Ladybird's still closed, he reasoned, he didn't have much else to do with his time. The meals he shared with the "good old boys' club" constituted the majority of his social life. Mavis didn't say too much about it, but it was obvious she found comfort in his presence. She had finally opened up to Ludie about her relationship with Melvin, and Ludie was not at all surprised to find that Mavis really cared about him. Ludie realized that the only reason Mavis had rejected Melvin was because she had already begun to suspect serious illness. Mavis didn't want to start a relationship knowing there might be something seriously wrong with her. Melvin hadn't given up, however, and was one of the first to be at her side when she was diagnosed. Ludie was glad he hadn't given up and that the two of them had found their way to each other at this stage of their lives.

Over the next couple of weeks, Ludie had given a great deal of thought to her own relationship. She made several attempts to discuss her concerns with Eric, but he either changed the subject each time, or blew off her accusations, as he called them, and attempted to turn the focus back on her. He accused her of not trusting him, of not being supportive of his career, and more.

Ludie started seeing Poppa more often. He had been at Birdie's during much of the holiday season, helping her clean up and get ready for re-opening, which was scheduled for New Year's Day. Poppa had become less reserved around Ludie, but she still couldn't help but see the sadness in his eyes when he thought she wasn't looking. He always greeted her with a hug and a kiss, but didn't seem as open to conversation as usual. It was painful knowing that he didn't approve, and she lacked the courage at this point to tell him he'd been right all along. Besides, she was holding out hope that she and Eric would be able to work things out. Eric had been busy with work. She was working at the shop and, with helping Mavis when Birdie was busy getting the café ready, it left them little time to iron things out together. All they needed was more time.

Brynn had told Ludie that sales would likely be dropping off dramatically after Christmas for a couple of weeks or so but then would gradually pick up again toward Valentine's Day. She asked Ludie to stay on at the shop part-time, knowing and understanding that her first loyalty was to Birdie. Ludie had happily agreed and was perfectly willing to work out a schedule that would be satisfactory to both Birdie and Brynn.

When it was opening day at the Ladybird, Ludie went to work early to help Birdie prepare. The diner was beautiful, and she couldn't help but take some pride in Eric's vision when she saw the finished product. It was New Year's Day, and Robert had cooked enough cornbread and black-eyed peas to feed half the town. Birdie and Ludie found themselves hoping half the town would show up. She had to hire some additional staff, considering the part-time teenage helpers that helped out before had moved on after the fire.

When they turned the open sign around in the front window, Ludie was pleasantly surprised to see so many of the regulars show up for lunch. Even the good ole boys' table filled up, with Melvin conspicuously absent. The customers were all pleased with the new look and said it had been worth the wait.

Shortly after the lunch crowd had thinned out, Ludie saw Melvin walking up to open the door. As he propped it open, Mavis stepped through. Ludie raced over to her and gave her a big hug.

"You look wonderful, Mavis!" she shouted, and Birdie and Robert were right behind her. After everyone had gushed over her a moment or two, Mavis looked around the room and smiled.

"I had to come and check out my new digs," she said, much to Ludie's surprise. "And of course, to pick up my schedule."

Birdie immediately commenced to fussing over her, much to Mavis's dismay. Mavis assured Birdie she was fine and demanded that she be

104

shown where they'd put her coffeemaker and all the dishes and condiments.

Mavis sat down with Birdie for a while and convinced her to let her work a couple hours every day until she could work her way back to a regular schedule.

"Fine," Birdie snapped. "But I'll be watching you. If I see you even *look* like you're feeling weak, that's it. You're sitting down or going home to rest."

Mavis explained that she had already shown great progress and that the oncologist had cleared her on the condition that she maintain a strict follow-up routine over the next few months as he'd carefully laid out. It would mean having scans done to ensure there was no re-growth of tumors and blood-work to ensure there were no serious changes. Ludie couldn't be happier with her news and managed to occupy her mind so fully with the grand re-opening and with Mavis's recovery that she was able to shove her problems with Eric to the back of her mind.

Things between them improved slightly over the next few weeks if, for no other reason, that both of them had managed to stay so busy with work. He'd not been so insensitive as to insult her again, at least not in the company of others, and she was grateful. With time she'd been able to accept that his behavior had been largely sparked by his heavy responsibilities and the resulting fatigue. Her tendency toward being overly sensitive hadn't helped, and she knew that. Thinking about it now embarrassed her.

# Chapter 9

The job at Katherine's house came to a close at the end of January, and Ludie was more relieved than she was willing to admit. It had seemed to take so long, and she couldn't imagine how a home could have taken more time and effort than an entire restaurant makeover. Nonetheless she was pleased, and willing to give their relationship her attentions and make it work. She was certainly not willing to give up so easily and risk having to face everyone with the admission that she had rushed into the relationship and had been wrong.

By the first week of February, she was feeling more tired than usual, but chalked it up to all the stress of recent events. When her fatigue was no longer her only symptom, she began to give it more consideration. One morning she woke up to the smell of coffee brewing in the kitchen, and was hit with a wave of nausea. Eric had gotten up before her and was already in the kitchen. She raced to the bathroom but stopped short of being sick. Standing at the sink, she washed her face with cool water and looked into the mirror. Horrified, it occurred to her that she was over a week late with her cycle. *How could I have not noticed?* she asked herself. She went back to the bed she shared with Eric and climbed in, pulling the covers up to her chin. She was expected at the diner this morning but couldn't fathom the idea of exposing herself to all the aromas of breakfast being cooked and served. She sent Birdie a text and let her know she wouldn't be making it in this morning due to a stomach bug, apologizing for the inconvenience.

Shortly afterward, she heard Eric's keys jingling and the front door close behind him. She got up and dressed quickly. Now that it had occurred to her she might be pregnant, she needed to know the truth. Making sure his car was gone, she grabbed her purse and keys and headed for the drugstore.

Less than half an hour later, she found herself scanning all the home pregnancy tests that lined the shelves. Some were an easy-to-read blue line; others guaranteed early results, up to ten days before the first missed period. She grabbed a couple of different ones, not wanting to take any chances of being mistaken. As she walked toward the checkout line, she realized the cashier looked vaguely familiar and conspicuously unoccupied at the moment. That meant she might be open to conversation, chatty even. She spent a few minutes hoping a line would form and she could inconspicuously blend into it. When it didn't, she put everything back where she'd gotten it and left without purchasing anything. *Humph*…. she thought, *and I thought I loved the fact that Blackwater's such a small town.*

Within the hour, she was in a larger, discount store several miles away, attempting to locate the same tests she had almost purchased at the drug store. This time, though, she found a self-check line that would mean not risking having anyone she knew ringing up her purchase. She couldn't risk drawing attention to her condition. Or *possible condition* she corrected herself.

When she walked in the front door at home she threw her purse on the sofa and ran straight for the bathroom, opening up the packages as she went. Her mind raced with the possibilities. What would she do? Would having a child together bring her and Eric closer together?

Pacing the floor she waited. "Hurry, hurry!" she urged the test stick. *Dear God,* she thought. Before the lines began to show even the faintest of color she heard the keys in the door.

"Ludie?" Eric called out to her. "Where are you?"

She swept everything off the counter in one motion except the test stick. She didn't want to move it and risk altering the test. She threw a hand-towel over it and answered him.

"In the bathroom!" she shouted. She heard him just outside the door.

"What's wrong?" he asked. "I went by Birdie's and you weren't there. She said you had a stomach bug?"

"Um, yea, it hit me pretty suddenly," she told him through the closed door. Her breathing came rapidly at the thought of being discovered or even worse, of having to lie to the man she loved. She opened the door to face him, guarding the towel, and the secret it buried, with her hip by leaning against it.

"You look awful," he told her, then apparently realized how that must have sounded and rushed to correct himself. "I mean, you look pale and clammy. Do you need anything? Maybe some ginger ale or crackers or anything?"

"No, babe," Ludie answered him, touched by his concern. "I just need to rest, I'll be all right. It's probably just a twenty-four hour thing." Her heart raced in her chest, knowing that a towel was the only thing between her and the answers that would decide the rest of her life, possibly.

She walked him to the door, terrified the whole time that he'd need to use the restroom and discover what she was hiding. Fortunately, he left, closing and locking the door behind him. She felt her eyes forming tears at his gesture of concern. Maybe, just maybe, she considered, he really did love her enough to take care of her.

Rushing back to the bathroom, she removed the towel while holding her breath. She felt herself reeling as she focused on the test. *Positive.* She looked down, rubbing her still-flat tummy with the palm of her hand. For a few moments, she considered the possibility that throwing the towel on top of the test stick had perhaps disturbed it, affecting the test. She opened the other package and followed the instructions, grateful that this time Eric didn't interrupt. It confirmed what she already knew. It was true. She was going to have a baby. She couldn't be alone right now, she knew, and she certainly didn't want to be there in her current state when Eric got home from work.

She went to the candle shop, hoping there were no customers. When she walked in the door it was just Brynn, and she was relieved. "Brynn," she cried, "I need to talk to you." She had barely taken a step into the work area when she was hit with an uncontrollable surge of nausea. Black cherry again.

"Honey, what is it?" she asked, taking her by the hand and leading her to the back, away from the prying eyes of any potential customers that might enter at any time.

Once Ludie allowed herself to give in to the tears, she quickly surrendered to heart-wrenching sobs. "I'm pregnant," she cried.

"Oh my goodness!" That's great!" Brynn answered, then hesitated. "Wait, isn't it?" Her brow creased with worry. "What did Eric say?"

"He doesn't know!" Ludie sobbed. "I couldn't tell him."

Brynn pulled out a chair near her desk for Ludie and then sat down across from her. "Why haven't you told him? How long have you known?"

Ludie explained to her that she'd just taken the test and that she couldn't tell Eric yet. This was the first time she had ever let on that things were less than perfect between her and Eric, and she noticed that Brynn didn't seem at all surprised.

"Honey, you've got to look inside and ask yourself why you didn't feel comfortable telling him."

The door chimed, indicating a customer. "I'm gonna' go out and take care of that; you just take your time. Wash your face, Sweetie, and come out when you're ready."

She went to the bathroom and washed her face, suppressing further waves of sobs, and then finally went to the front. It was Roxy. She heard her voice before she'd even come around the corner.

"Hello, Luv. Where's Ludie? She hasn't returned my calls today."

"I'm here," Ludie said softly, walking toward them.

"Bloody hell, Luv!" she exclaimed. "What happened to you?"

At that, Ludie burst into tears. She felt the comforting embrace of a group hug, and before she knew it, she'd told the whole story. She told them just how bad things had gotten with Eric, and about the pregnancy and how there were so many variables at the moment.

"Well," snapped Roxy. "You sure as hell don't need a bloody bloke to help you have that baby. If he's not treating you like you deserve what's to make you think he'll take proper care of a baby?" Her bright copper red hair burned with gleams that matched the fire in her eyes. She was furious.

Another round of sobs threatened, and Roxy quickly added, "That's what you've got us for, Luv. You'll not go through this alone. It's time to put that man in his place!" The two women immediately began making plans and discussing them, including everything from delivery coaching to paying for college. They made it clear she wouldn't face this alone. While they planned and discussed, Ludie sat and quietly wept.

She felt torn apart, knowing that although Eric hadn't been very attentive as of late, this was his child and she owed it to herself and her baby to try to make it work. As much as she appreciated her friends she knew this was a decision she would have to make on her own with as little outside influence as possible.

After a lengthy talk, she told them both she needed to go home and get her thoughts together. She excused herself, thanking them both, and went to the apartment to collect her thoughts. She'd simply have to tell him, she decided, and let the chips fall where they may. Surely once he knew there was a baby on the way he would embrace the idea. He would surely be gentler with her once he knew she was pregnant.

When she got home, she quickly undressed and stepped into the shower, enjoying the warm water flowing over her body. She lingered there, her thoughts circling around her situation, rehearsing and forming the words she would tell Eric.

Stepping out, she dried off and dressed in her soft terry cloth robe. She ran a brush through her hair, and inhaled sharply. It was almost time for Eric to get home and she would be waiting. When he finally came through the door she could tell he'd had at least a couple of drinks. He had that slightly rumpled look she had grown accustomed to, with the all-too-familiar smell of alcohol on his breath. He put down his phone and keys, and reached into a kitchen drawer and removed a corkscrew. He opened a bottle of wine and poured a glass, leaning against the bar. She remained perched on the bar stool where she'd been sitting and watched him.

He eyed her carefully. She was up to something, and he knew it. His thoughts were of his long and difficult day and that he didn't need to come home to the scrutiny of a little girl which, for all practical purposes, she was. He knew what was coming because he'd heard it all before. *Where have you been? Who were you with?* He was in no mood for it.

"All right," he said, his speech slightly slurred. "What's going on?"

She hesitated briefly, debating on whether or not this was a good time to share her news. Perhaps it would be better to wait until he hadn't been drinking, she thought, although it occurred to her that she'd likely already be showing by the time that ever happened.

"Eric," she said, pausing to gather her strength. "How do you feel about us?" she drew in some air. "I mean, where do you see us going?"

He drew his brows together and clenched his jaw in concentration. "I don't know," he answered slowly, piercing her heart. "I guess things are going okay," he said. "Why? Where is this coming from?"

Glaring at him she threw some of his words

back at him. "Okay? You guess?" she said slowly, rising to her feet. "Eric, whatever happened to us having a future? It was *your* idea for me to move in here! What's changed?"

He pressed the rim of the glass to his lips and tilted it back to empty the last few drops, setting it down slowly. He met her gaze. "I don't know. Sometimes things just change." He flashed a sadistic smile, as if he enjoyed her discomfort.

Feeling her world slip out from beneath her, she gripped the bar. Tears filled her eyes, and another wave of nausea swept over her. "What's changed?" she pressed. "Katherine? Having drinks in the city with the boys? What?"

He leaned against the bar, studying her with thinly-veiled amusement. "What's all this about?" he asked again. "I have a life and a career. You knew that coming into this."

She straightened, drawing on her reserves of strength. "What do you want out of life, Eric? What are your goals?"

"You know what my goals are. Building my business, making a profit, hiring more hands."

"I'm not talking about work, Eric," she hissed. "What about marriage, and family?"

He chuckled under his breath. "Marriage? Maybe someday," he said. "I haven't given it much thought." Setting the wine glass in the sink he sauntered to the refrigerator and opened it, surveying its contents as if they'd been casually discussing the weather.

"Well, we don't have until 'someday,'" she said. "We barely have nine months."

114

At this, he straightened abruptly and closed the refrigerator door, turning to face her. His square jaw tensed visibly. "What are you saying?"

"I'm pregnant, Eric. We're going to have a baby." She felt the air leaking from her lungs and wondered how much longer she'd be able to continue breathing. His glare burned through her. She felt her life slipping away, her dreams deflating faster than her lungs. A hollow pang spread from the center of her chest, threatening what little confidence she had left.

He met her gaze sharply. "We're not ready," he said simply. "There's a lot to consider first, before either of us starts making decisions about whether or not to have a family in the future."

"The future? The *future?*" she demanded. "This baby is not in the distant future, Eric! It's coming, in just a few months, like it or not."

"Ludie," he said, speaking slowly and deliberately as if he were explaining grown-up things to a small child, "this is not the right time. We'll see a doctor, it would probably be best to see someone in Houston. They deal with this kind of thing all day every day and are much more experienced. You'll be in better hands there." He smiled condescendingly, as if he were doing her a huge favor by even discussing this with her. "I'll even take you myself."

"You don't even know if you want a life with me!" she shouted. "I'm sure as hell not going to let you be a part of choosing my obstetrician! I don't even *want* you there."

He turned back to face her again. "Obstetrician?" he asked. "Ludie, we need to get on the same page here. You're not having this baby." He said it as matter-of-factly as if he were telling her she wasn't going to pick up the dry cleaning. "Neither of us needs this right now."

With that, what felt like the last remaining air slipped from her lungs. She went into the bedroom and slammed the door. Opening the closet, she removed one of her bags and began furiously throwing clothes into it. It took all the concentration she could muster to pull air into her lungs without gasping. She dressed quickly and, moments later, emerged from the bedroom, her face set in unwavering determination. "I'm having this baby," she said. "I don't need your help. You can just carry on with your life and whatever interests you. But I'm having this baby."

"You don't tell me when *I'm* going to be a father. It's not something you just *decide* for me," he said, his dark eyes boring into her. He spoke with contempt that forbade any further argument. She opened the apartment door and stepped out into the hallway, pausing at the top of the stairs to shift the weight of her suitcase. It happened so quickly she wasn't sure if she could have stopped him if she'd seen it coming. He crossed the room in what seemed like a single step and threw the door back so hard it thrust the door knob into the wall.

She felt his hands on her so quickly and for a split second she thought he was going to pull her back into the apartment and maybe into his

116

arms. In that brief lightning fast moment she thought maybe he had come to his senses and realized what was at stake.

She looked up into his face in time to see it twisted with rage and, without enough time to brace herself, she attempted to take a single step down. She felt the very back edge of her heel hit the edge of the step, and felt herself falling. She tumbled fast, feeling each step so hard, yet each move unfolded slowly, freakishly, until she hit the bottom step. The spasms in her abdomen hit so quickly, so furiously, that before she hit the bottom step she already knew it was over. Over before it started. Clutching her stomach she cried out, protectively folding herself into her middle. Fear gripped her heart as she saw him racing down, taking the steps two at a time.

"Ludie!" he shouted. "Let me help you! If I had seen you falling in time I would have caught you." *How quickly things change*, she thought bitterly.

"It's just that you were running away from me so fast, I could hardly reach you..." he continued. Breathless, he leaned over her, his face clouded with worry.

"Reach me? *Reach* me?" she hissed through clenched teeth, still clutching her belly. "You were the reason I fell!"

"No, no, I only wanted to talk some sense into you, I never meant for you to fall!" he moaned. "Let me help you upstairs, and let you catch your breath. You're upset." He grasped her hand and attempted to help her to her feet.

"Take your hands off me," she demanded through gritted teeth, gathering more strength than she knew she had. "I 'fell' down the stairs, Eric. As long as you take your hands off me and let me leave here on my own, that's my story, beginning to end." Her eyes fixed on his, showing her determination.

He slowly unfolded his fingers from her arms, backing away as recognition crossed his face. Realizing she had the upper hand and not willing to take any further risks, his face took on a threatening expression.

"One word, Ludie. You tell *one* person anything other than that, and life as you know it will be over. I will know, and I will find you." His black eyes burned into her, sharp and unwavering. She clenched her jaw to kill the sob she felt building in her throat. Grasping the railing on the stairs she pulled herself to her feet. Reaching for her bag, she pulled it up by the handle and pulled it behind her on its wheels. He took it from her hand and threw it into the cab of her truck.

Again, he gave her a cold, hard look. "I meant what I said. You'll be a whole lot safer if you keep that in mind."

She sat in the truck, fully realizing she would be so much better off without him. Better to learn that lesson now than later, when she would have invested so much more.

As she drove away into the night she felt more spasms wrack her abdomen.

# Chapter 10

Ludie wouldn't be able to make it all the way out to the farm in this condition. The cramps stabbed from deep within her lower abdomen. Besides, what would she tell Poppa? She couldn't just show up at the hospital, either. No, it was better to stay close, with someone she could trust to keep quiet for now. Pulling up at Roxy's house a few blocks away, she leaned into the horn long enough to let her know she was there. She looked up seconds later to see the blinds part slightly, and then the front door open.

"What in bloody hell?" her friend asked, closing the distance between her front door and Ludie's truck. "Ah, hell, Luv," she said. "We've got to get you some help."

Ludie wasn't ready to talk about it, telling her friend that she'd fallen down the stairs and that Eric wasn't home at the time so she came to her for help. Roxy had helped her to her car, closing the door for her. As she drove her to the hospital, Ludie made her promise she'd take her to the larger hospital down the freeway.

Roxy argued that it was further away and that she needed to go straight to Blackwater Memorial to get more immediate help. Ludie reminded her that no one knew she was pregnant and she didn't want small town rumors to fly so

119

quickly that her Poppa would find out. She couldn't bear to bring him any more pain by letting him know he'd lost a great-grandchild. Roxy had agreed that made sense, and wasted no time getting her to the larger hospital in Seaview.

When they pulled up to the emergency room entrance Roxy raced to the automatic sliding doors and demanded a wheelchair. Within moments they'd assisted her into the chair and taken her into a room. Ludie continued to sob quietly, not only for the loss of the life she'd hoped to have with Eric, but for the lost child she'd only had a single day to dream of. Again, she grabbed her middle protectively, and waited.

A nurse came into the room and gently explained the procedure to her. A technician come to take her for a fetal ultrasound, and gave permission for Roxy to accompany her. As she lay on the cold table, she felt the heated ultrasound gel ooze onto her belly. Softly weeping, she prepared herself for what was ahead.

Looking up into the face of the technician, she saw his expression change. He moved the smooth, rounded device across her abdomen and refocused on the screen. His eyebrows lifted as he again moved across and lower.

He excused himself briefly and she heard him speak into a phone just at the edge of the doorway. "Yea, this is Matt in ultrasound. I've got an OB transfer," he said.

Turning back to her, he made his way back for another look. She looked up at him, terrified.

"What does that mean? You need OB? They have to do something to me? Is that how they handle miscarriages?" He seemed embarrassed that she'd overheard his phone conversation, and then surprised by his words.

"Miscarriage?" He again moved the probe across her middle and pointed to a small pulsating white spot on the screen. "I can't really give results on anything, and I can't tell you what's in store. But what I *can* tell you is that this is a heartbeat."

Ludie turned to look at Roxy, whose red-lipsticked mouth formed a small "O." *A heartbeat.* She didn't think it was possible after what she'd just endured!

Quickly she reminded herself not to get her hopes up or to read anything into this. She'd taken a horrible fall, or so she'd need to tell everyone. A baby so tiny wasn't likely to survive such a trauma, she told herself, bracing for what was surely inevitable.

The technician smiled sadly at her, clearly unsure of how to respond to her changing emotions. Roxy had moved from her chair nearby and was leaning over Ludie, holding her hand and looking into her eyes, lending comfort and hoping to encourage her to be strong for what she could be facing.

Ludie took a sharp breath, unable to take her eyes from the screen. It looked like the tiniest of jelly beans. *How could something so tiny have a heartbeat?* she wondered, and commenced to brace herself and be ready. She could do this, she knew. She had the support of her friends and would no doubt have the added support of Birdie and Poppa if the situation called for it. For the second time today waiting to hear the news that would change her life forever, she dropped her head back to the pillow and just focused on the task of breathing in and out. The technician began cleaning off the smooth rounded end of the device and clicking the screen to apparently save the shots for the physician.

They kept Ludie overnight to observe her, but had assured her that her baby was still showing a strong heartbeat, at least for the time being. They explained that as early on as it was in the pregnancy, there were no guarantees, especially after taking such a hard fall. Roxy stayed with her overnight. The next morning, after discussing it with Ludie, she called Brynn, who arrived at the hospital shortly thereafter.

"Dear God, what on earth?" she shouted, storming into the room, throwing her purse on the bedside table. "Why didn't you call me?"

"Relax, Susie Sunshine. You'll scare her to death," Roxy snapped.

Brynn immediately began to rattle off questions, more than Ludie knew how to answer. She had questions on fetal age, measurements, things Ludie knew nothing about. It just so happened that conveniently Brynn was in her semester of labor and delivery and was studying prenatal care. Ludie wasn't sure if that would ultimately be a blessing or a curse.

"What does Eric think? Did you end up

telling him?" Brynn asked, looking around and opening the door to the bathroom. "Where is he?"

Ludie's eyes immediately filled, and within seconds she was suppressing a fresh round of tears. Roxy elbowed her in the ribs. "Way to go, Luv. Now you've got her going again."

Ludie looked down, knowing she would eventually have to level with them both. "He's not here," she said, "and he won't be." She then went on to enlighten them both about what had really happened on the stairs.

Both of them leaned in and said, virtually at the same time, "What?"

Ludie took in a sharp breath and made them both promise not to tell anyone and not to react impulsively. Once assured that her secrets would be safe, she began to tell them the details.

Brynn reacted more slowly and logically, as Ludie had hoped. Roxy, however, was ballistic, forcing Brynn to close the door and attempt to calm her down. "Dammit, Brynn!" she hissed.

Ludie didn't know whether to laugh or cry at the sight of her two friends fussing over how to handle the news. It was all so overwhelming to her that it might be a good distraction to have these two performing.

The reality of the situation hadn't sunk in, and she was still trying to wrap her head around the pregnancy, let alone the idea that it was threatened. When the nurse came in to discuss her discharge instructions, the two excited visitors hushed to listen. Based on the instructions, she was to go home and rest for a couple of days to avoid causing any further uterine irritability. They placed her on what was referred to as "pelvic rest," which meant she was to refrain from sexual activity, at least until she was out of danger of miscarrying. She choked back a bitter sob. After a brief discussion of where she would go, it was decided she would stay at Brynn's so that she could keep an eye on her. Roxy wasn't pleased and made that fact known, but she had to admit, she knew nothing about prenatal care and Brynn obviously did.

When they got to Brynn's, Ludie went straight to the soft, plush sofa and sat down, putting her feet up. The two began to make a fuss over her and, before long, the subject turned to Eric. Since Ludie had told them the full story, they had both remained livid. Ludie had minimized his bad behavior for a while, but it was clear her friends wouldn't be minimizing anything. Roxy took Ludie's key and went to pick up as many of Ludie's belongings as she could while Eric was at work. She made quick work of it in order to avoid having to confront him. Ludie thought that was a wise decision. Eric would be lucky to avoid her angry friend. Roxy wasn't pleasant to deal with when she was a woman scorned. She was furious with Eric. She didn't know him, but she despised him already and had been very vocal about plotting her revenge. He would not get away with this, Roxy vowed, and Ludie and Brynn didn't have the strength to argue with her at that point.

When Roxy had delivered the items she'd collected for her from Eric's apartment, she had come in to discover Ludie still sleeping on the couch. Leaning over and giving her a kiss on the forehead, she vowed to avenge this sweet girl who had been hurt so badly. Brynn was at the shop, but had left a note to let her know what time she'd be home and the numbers to reach her if she needed anything. Satisfied that Brynn had covered her bases and would be home shortly, Roxy let herself out quietly.

Ludie awoke several hours later, relieved that she had finally been able to get some sleep with no further cramps. Her first thoughts were of the child growing inside her, and then they quickly turned to Eric. She had such high hopes, and had dreamt of a future with him. What had she been thinking? Why hadn't she seen this coming? Every time he hurt her feelings or upset her, he'd always managed to sooth her. Each time she considered leaving him, he would say or do something so thoughtful, so endearing, that it had more than made up for what he'd done to hurt her. And each time, she fell for it, more hopelessly in love than she'd been before.

This time, though, there would be no making up for it. Eric had hurt her beyond repair, because when he rejected her baby, *his* baby, he rejected her. She placed the palm of her hand gently on her lower abdomen, her thoughts swirling, wondering about the tiny life growing inside her. Determined, she grimly made up her mind to start a new life for herself and her child.

Unable to imagine how she would deal with this, she resolved to herself that she would be strong for her baby. What Eric's involvement might be, she didn't know. She wasn't sure if she even wanted him to know. She'd be better off without him, she knew that now.

A key turned in the lock, interrupting her thoughts. Ben opened the door and stepped into the foyer. As soon as he noticed her, he threw his keys on the entry table and rushed to her side. Taking a seat on the chair near where she was lying, he asked her what was wrong. Unsure of how much to tell him, she sighed deeply and told him what had happened. Most of it, anyway. As protective as he was of those he cared about, she didn't dare tell him Eric had been advancing toward her in such a threatening manner when she fell. Ben had treated her so well since she'd been working for Brynn, thanking her for being supportive of his sister every time they worked together. Oh what she wouldn't give to have a brother like him. She hoped her friend was grateful and knew how blessed she was.

"It's over between us," she whispered, feeling her eyes fill with tears yet again. "He doesn't want me to have the baby. He says if I do, then we're finished." She swallowed the despair she felt rising in her throat.

"You're finished anyway," Ben replied. "He doesn't deserve you, Ludie, he never did." She was surprised by his concern, not knowing he had ever given her relationship with Eric any thought.

"Then why does it hurt so much? Why did I think we had a future?" she asked softly. "He's not as bad as I'm making him sound. There have been so many good days, Ben." She didn't know why, but she wanted so badly for Ben to believe her. Perhaps it was because she didn't want anyone to think that the only real relationship she'd ever had was a complete disaster. It was humbling to realize the only man who had ever loved her could be so cruel and selfish. Somehow she needed to cling to the good memories; those sweet moments they'd shared had made her feel special.

"He had a good woman, and he blew it," Ben said. "Stop making excuses for him." His eyes bore into hers, and she almost felt as though she was burning under his scrutiny.

She pulled the blanket up to her chin and rested her head against the back of the couch. It was flattering that Ben felt the way he did, and she appreciated his kindness, but there was no way she could make him understand what she'd had with Eric.

"What are you going to do about the baby?" he asked. "I mean, what are the chances..." he trailed off, uncertain how to phrase the question without being insensitive.

"I'm not completely out of danger," Ludie told him. "They said it's so early, and I fell hard. That's why they have me on bed rest. Even though I've only known about the baby for one day, I don't want to lose it. In just over twenty-four hours, I've already started talking to it," she admitted sadly. "As for what I'll do, I don't know. I can't imagine how I'll tell my grandfather. He'll be so disappointed in me."

At this, Ben reacted strongly. "You are *not* a disappointment, and I hope I never hear you say that again. This is not your fault, Ludie. You got hurt, it happens to the best of us but it doesn't speak any less of you. You'll be a great mother." His smile was soft, reassuring.

"If I'm a mother at all," she said, tears filling her eyes again.

"If not this time, then one day," he said simply. His eyes shone with sincerity. Sincere, she thought. That was the best way to describe Ben. She warmed at the comfort his concern brought her.

Bringing himself to his feet he leaned over her, adjusting the blanket to cover her feet, which were propped on the ottoman in front of her. "Is there anything I can get for you?"

"No, I'm fine. Thank you. Brynn made me something to eat before she went to the shop. I've been instructed not to leave the couch unless I absolutely have to."

"That's my sister for you," he laughed. "She's always been bossy, so don't take it personally." After their talk, she felt better. Her future was hanging in the air, her emotions swirling, but she was comforted knowing she had such a wonderful circle of support. Her gratitude for such good friends was nearly overwhelming.

When Brynn came home, she immediately began asking questions. "Have you had any bleeding? Cramps?"

"No, I've just been resting, and slept for a long time."

"Good. Good," Brynn said. "You just stay right there, I'm going to make you some dinner in a little bit. Where's Ben?"

"He just got in from work a little while ago," she answered. "He went down the hall to take a shower."

"He's going to pick Blake up from school for me later. He has a late day, yearbook committee, I think."

"He's lucky to have such a great uncle. Ben's great, Brynn. I hope you realize how blessed you are to have a brother like him."

"I do. Blake loves having him living here with us. It's been good for him, especially since his father has never really been in the picture." Ludie's thoughts again turned to Eric, and what his involvement would be if this baby survived. She even found herself briefly wondering if they'd just gone through a rough patch and could possibly work things out.

That evening, Roxy came back over and they all had dinner together. It was informal, hot dogs and macaroni and cheese, and they ate in the living room on TV trays. After they'd finished eating, Ludie got up and excused herself to the bathroom. As soon as she stood up, she felt a sharp pain deep in her pelvic region. Raw, desolate grief overwhelmed her, and she bit her lip until it throbbed like her pulse. Brynn rushed to her side to help.

Ben's face showed his concern, but Blake was oblivious due to his uncle's quick thinking. He distracted him by snatching the remote and clicking.

"Let's find some sports, buddy, no more of this chick stuff."

Ludie made it down the hall, gingerly taking one step at a time. Moments later, Ludie sat on the toilet, leaning forward and clutching her belly. Brynn was wiping her face with a cool cloth and speaking soothingly to her. She wanted so badly to be able to tell her it was all going to be okay and the baby would be fine, but she knew that would be more painful for her in the long run. She feared her friend's cramps meant the worst, and knew that right then she had to find the right blend of compassion and reality.

"Sweetie, I need you to relax as much as you can. Take some deep breaths, okay?" She held her hand, and breathed with her, helping her to pace her breaths in a slower, more rhythmic pattern.

Ludie began taking slow, deep breaths, in through her nose and out through her mouth. Just then she was seized with pain that jolted her, along with a wave of nausea. She felt something warm and sticky between her legs, and a terrified expression crossed her face. She took some tissue and wiped gently, and as she held it out and saw the bright red blood, she felt Brynn's arms wrapped around her, holding her while she cried.

# Chapter 11

They returned to the hospital, where they repeated a pelvic exam and assessment. The doctor assured her it was most likely that her body would be able to naturally expel the blood and tissue and that she would probably not require a "D and C," or dilation and curettage. Although it was meant as assurance, Ludie couldn't help but cringe at the terminology. Her heart ached for what might have been. The nurse gave them instructions for her care and what to expect, and urged her to return if there was any fever or other signs of infection. It was decided she would return to Brynn's so she could look after her until it was certain that she was not in any danger of infection or hemorrhage.

Brynn drove home, while Ludie sat in the passenger seat and wept. Brynn did her best to comfort her friend, but knew that it would take time for her to heal.

"I'm so sorry, baby. It shouldn't be like this," Brynn said, reaching over to squeeze her hand. Ludie looked over at her and gave a weak smile.

She knew she was young and would have other chances, provided she ever met the right person and was given that chance. She'd only known for one day, one single day, and yet the pain was there as if she'd planned for nine months. Was it supposed to be like *this?* She wondered.

When they arrived home, Roxy's car was in the driveway. They could make out her figure in the driver's seat. She was waiting for them. When they parked and got out, the two women walked on either side of her as they went into the house. At Brynn's insistence, Ludie sat on the most comfortable recliner and leaned back, trying to relax. They had given her a mild sedative at the hospital, so she took some deep breaths and allowed herself to yield to its effects.

As her emotions roiled throughout her, she thought of Poppa and how hurt he'd be if he knew. She couldn't bear to disappoint him, and she vowed then and there never to tell him. She knew her secret would be safe with her friends. She'd tell Birdie she needed a couple more days to recover from a stomach virus and knew she'd give her the time she needed. It was no secret that Birdie was a close friend of the family and held a special affection for Ludie. It would just mean less heartbreak to keep this secret.

"You'll need to be a hundred percent when you do come back," Birdie said when she called her. "I've got some teenagers hired to handle the increase in business, and I'll need you as an interpreter," she laughed. "How is it they're not much younger than you were when you first came to work for me? They don't have half the work ethic you do." Birdie went on talking excitedly about the new and improved Ladybird Cafe. Ludie let her continue, not wanting to ruin her moment. She was honored that Birdie valued her and trusted her enough that she'd even asked her to train the new employees and take charge. When she hung up the phone, she was grateful to have Ladybird's to keep her busy in the coming weeks. She heard Roxy and Brynn in the other room speaking in hushed tones in order to allow her to rest. She smiled at the thought of how protective they were, and how good it felt to have a couple of mother hens to nurture her. *Mother.* The very thought of the word brought a new wave of tears and she quietly let them fall and eventually drifted off to sleep.

When Ben and Blake came home later, she awoke to the sound of them coming through the door. She and Ben exchanged glances and she knew at that moment that he'd been told it was definitely a miscarriage. Strangely, she found it comforting, and somehow it made her feel safer knowing that he knew.

The boys had brought home pizzas for dinner, and again they all ate in the living room, insisting that Ludie stay in the recliner with her feet up. Brynn hovered and Ludie let her. Roxy had stayed for dinner, and the two of them never left her alone for more than a few minutes the entire evening.

Ludie's phone had been going off all evening, and Roxy had finally taken it from her and turned the ringer off. Eric had hit her with a barrage of calls and text messages. She had been able to read a few of them before Roxy took her phone, and had been strangely gratified at his concern. Even though she knew there would be no future with him, she was glad he was worried, and then she wondered if his worries were genuinely for her or for himself. He knew she had a strong support system in this town and that it wasn't going to bode well for him or his business here if it became known that he was the one who caused this. She drew a certain amount of sick satisfaction at knowing that.

Ludie looked up to see Roxy sending a text message, her thumbs flying furiously over the screen. When Ludie gave her a sharp look, Roxy shrugged and responded with a sheepish look. Ludie held her hand out for the phone and Roxy grudgingly gave it back to her. The message read:

*Ludie can't return your calls at this time. She's in Houston and in critical condition. She's being interviewed by hospital officials at the moment and it's best you not continue to contact her.*

"Roxy!" Ludie said sharply. "Why did you do that?"

"The bastard needs to sweat a little, don't you think?" With that, Roxy stood and said she needed to go and get some things done. She reminded Brynn yet again to call her if Ludie needed anything. Leaning over to give Ludie a kiss on the cheek she told her to take things slowly and to rest as much as she could.

As much as Ludie wanted to be angry with her for interfering, she did get at least a little

134

satisfaction knowing he'd be worried. She and Brynn even managed to laugh a bit wondering what Eric was doing at that moment. Ludie found herself hoping he was looking over his shoulder and waiting for the police.

Ludie had opted not to report him to the police even though she'd been encouraged by her friends to do so. He hadn't actually hit her, she reasoned, and besides, it was a small enough town that word would quickly get to Birdie and then to Poppa. Word always traveled fast in the good old boys' network and she couldn't bear to hurt her loved ones any more than she already had by her actions.

After she rested for a couple of days, she grew restless and longed to return to work. Her friends had been fabulous and she would remain ever grateful for their care, but the more time she took lying around the more she thought about what had happened.

When Ludie returned to work at Birdie's she was greeted with a quick hug and an apron tossed at her. She laughed, glad that she wasn't going to be fussed over so much. She needed to feel normal again, whatever that was.

"Ludie, this is Tyler and Courtney. They're gonna' be helping out," Birdie said. "I know you can show them the ropes and get them acquainted with how we do things around here." Stepping away to answer to a customer who was flagging her down, she looked over her shoulder at the two overwhelmed teenagers. "See that you listen to her," Birdie instructed them.

Mavis came in around lunchtime and worked during the lunch rush. She took it slow, taking only two or three tables at a time, relying on Ludie and her two new shadows to do a great deal of the legwork. Her hair was starting to grow back and Ludie was pleased to see that she didn't bother to disguise it any longer with a hat or turban. She had some really cute earrings and, as always, a pencil behind her ear. Ludie called her to the storeroom in back to have a few words with her. She told her how proud she was of her for fighting and winning her battle. The two embraced, and Ludie got the strong feeling that Mavis sensed there was something different about her. This was certainly not the time to bring it up, she knew, but considered the possibility that she would one day need to confide in her. Mavis was so very wise, and never judgmental.

Eric had eased off the phone calls but did send an occasional text message saying he hoped she was feeling better and to let him know if there was anything he could do. *Hah,* she thought. *As if he hadn't already done enough.* She didn't respond and felt fairly confident he wouldn't have the nerve to show up at the café. Although with his narcissism he was probably dying to see everyone's reaction to the new and improved cafe. Ludie gained some satisfaction knowing he wouldn't be able to have his ego stroked by all the praise.

She had to admit, there was a lot of talk around the café and the customers were mightily impressed. She smiled smugly knowing he wouldn't benefit from it.

Tyler and Courtney were joined at the hip and apparently intimidated by Birdie, as neither one of them hardly took a step without the other. If someone needed butter from the cooler, they both went. If there was trash to be taken to the back, they both went. Ludie knew that wouldn't work with Birdie and told them as much. She spent the better part of the afternoon showing them where everything was and, when they were out of Birdie's earshot, instructed them on how to deal with the boss. That, of course, proved to be the most valuable aspect of their training.

That evening after work Ludie went to the farmhouse. Poppa was out in the yard and looked up when he heard the tires of her truck crunching on the gravel. He had started toward the driveway by the time she parked and got out. When he hugged her, she felt his lack of enthusiasm. She had hurt him, and owed him some explanation.

"I'm glad to see you," she told him, walking toward the porch next to him.

"I haven't gone anywhere," he snapped. Realizing how sharp his answer was, he softened his tone. "I'm glad to see you, too."

In the warmth of the little kitchen he put on a pot of coffee. Poppa could drink coffee around the clock, Ludie mused. When it had finished brewing, she poured them both a cup. Opening the refrigerator door out of habit, she felt a twinge of pain when she saw a brand new bottle of her vanilla creamer on the top shelf, unopened. *He never gave up on me,* she thought. *He knew I would come home.*

Seated at the table across from him, she smiled at the comfort of the farmhouse's cozy kitchen. The slightly detectable scent from the gas stove blended with the always-present aroma of fresh coffee, and the ticking of Nanny's rooster clock made for a comforting and familiar atmosphere. She missed this place. It had been her home for nearly as long as she could remember and she was wrong to avoid it.

Sparing Poppa as many of the painful details as possible, she told him that she and Eric weren't working out. His bushy eyebrows lifted in response, but he resisted the urge to say "I told you so." He was hurt, and she knew it. He and Nanny had instilled certain values in her and she was thankful for their efforts and the love they'd shown her. It was difficult for her to come to terms with the way she'd thrown caution to the wind and dismissed those values.

"I don't suppose you want to come back to your old room anytime soon," Poppa mumbled, busying himself with folding, stacking and restacking newspapers on the table in order to not have to make eye contact with her.

Rising to her feet Ludie took a step toward him and leaned over, giving him a hug. "I love you, Poppa," she said. "I want to come home." She never expected to see tears in his eyes and, in an effort to not draw attention to them, she got up and rinsed her cup. It felt good to be home, she thought, but it would take a while to restore her relationship with Poppa. He never once told her how wrong she'd been about Eric and her decision to move, and she admired him for that. It must have taken all the resolve he had to keep from mentioning it.

That night, alone up in her old room, she found herself recalling her time with Eric. His romantic gestures, the way he looked at her, and the way he was so protective of her. *But who's going to protect me from him?* she wondered later that night as she drifted off to a troubled sleep.

*She heard the truck sputtering and looked down to see the gas gauge on empty. How had she let that happen? She never let it get that low. She kept pushing the accelerator and willing the truck to pick up speed, but it wouldn't. Finally, it choked to a stop and she surveyed her surroundings. She was at the bridge over Blackwater Creek. There was no one within a mile. Did she dare walk? Sage advice always warned never to leave a stranded vehicle alone.*

*Just then, a pair of bright headlights appeared over the horizon. As they grew closer, she realized it was Eric's car. She had to get away from the truck before he got close enough to recognize her. Her legs turned to rubber more and more with each step. Now, cement. She heard his car come to a halt just as she made it to the tree-line. The cypress trees drooped low, the moss hanging like flaccid arms and gnarled fingers, swaying in the wind. She feared if she came too close they would clutch her in their grasp. The fog rose from the soggy ground, hiding the swampy mud below. Her feet sunk into the wet, greedy marshland mud, pulling her down. A splash sounded nearby. An alligator, she guessed, but she was unable to visualize it in the dark of the night. She struggled to free herself, and felt herself falling. The ground smacked her hard when she hit, and she was writhing to turn over when she felt a hand reach out and grip her ankle. Eric stood over her; his malicious grin was sobering. The blade of a knife flashed in the reflection of the moonlight as he lunged toward her.*

She gave a choked scream and sat up straight in her bed. It was a dream. Eric wasn't really there. She was home in her bed. At the farm. No longer able to sleep, she got up and wrapped a blanket around her shoulders. She padded down the stairs quietly so as not to wake Poppa. In the kitchen, she put on a kettle for tea. It was hours before she was calm enough to return to bed, and finally sleep overtook her.

The next morning when things slowed down at the Ladybird, she walked down to the candle shop and told Brynn about how things had gone with Poppa.

"I'm glad," Brynn told her. "I found myself halfway hoping you'd stay a little longer, but I know you need to be at the farmhouse." She laughed aloud. "Besides, we both know Eric won't show up out there and take the risk of facing the barrel of your Poppa's shotgun." Ludie laughed as well.

"He's a coward, Ludie." Brynn looked up at her intently. "He won't hurt you, again, you know.

He wouldn't take that kind of chance. He's all mighty and powerful when it's just the two of you, but if he had to face anyone else, he'd back down."

"I know. I do. But I still feel like I have to look over my shoulder everywhere I go."

"After Roxy talked to Dennis," Brynn laughed, "I doubt he'll be around long." Ludie gave her a quick, sharp look.

"What do you mean Roxy talked to Dennis? Dennis, the firefighter?"

"Um, well, you know they've gone out to dinner a couple of times, right? He really likes her, and she doesn't know what she wants other than to have a good time. Dennis has already promised her the moon, but it's not the moon she wants. She wants Eric run out of town on a rail, and it wouldn't be beyond the realm of possibility."

At Ludie's reaction, Brynn was quick to console her.

"Don't worry, our secret's safe with Dennis. He's not going to do anything crazy." She flashed a smug grin. "But," she continued, "he *is* in charge of passing electrical inspections for the fire department. I'm just saying, it's going to be really sad when Eric's building permits don't get approved and he starts losing bids. All his city connections won't amount to a hill of beans."

At this revelation, Ludie couldn't help but laugh, forcing herself to trust that Dennis wouldn't talk to the good old boys' club. She didn't want to hurt Poppa with the knowledge of just how badly Eric had hurt her.

Changing the subject, she asked about how things were going at the shop. They penciled out a tentative schedule and Ludie went back to the café to wind down the day and help Birdie and Robert clean up. After dismissing the "scaredy-cat twins," as Birdie had dubbed Tyler and Courtney, they closed for the day.

# Chapter 12

It was only two days later when Ludie saw Eric for the first time since their breakup. She was walking down the sidewalk to a shop near the corner where the law firm beneath his apartment was located. She had made her purchases and had just stepped out onto the sidewalk when she almost collided with him. He seemed more surprised than she was, and he grabbed her shoulders with both hands in an attempt to keep her from fleeing.

"Ludie," he said. He seemed almost out of breath. "I've wanted to talk to you, there is so much…" He trailed off as she stepped back, causing him to release his hold on her.

"There's nothing left to say," she told him. "It's done, and *I'm* done."

"I was upset," he uttered breathlessly. "That night, I was just, it was a shock. We hadn't even had time to get used to the idea of each other, let alone a baby." At this, his brows drew together in a worried frown. "I mean, are you…. did…" he looked down, not finishing his question. She caught the unmistakable stench of alcohol on his breath, and noted his rumpled, unkempt appearance. He looked as though he hadn't slept well.

"No, Eric, I'm not," she snapped. "I lost the

baby that next day." She stepped to the right, attempting to walk past him. He blocked her, and then blocked her again when she stepped to the left. "Let me go," she hissed, through clenched teeth. "I will press charges if you don't leave me alone."

"Did you tell anyone?" Eric asked her. "Does anyone know about our fights?" He seemed truly worried now, and she found herself strangely satisfied at that revelation.

"Our fights?" she asked. "Is that how you see it? Because what I remember is you bullying me, and charging at me like a maniac. I was scared of you and that's why I fell." Her courage and determination provided the resolve she needed to say those things.

"That's not how it happened and you know it. And whatever it is you *think* I've done to you is *nothing* compared to what I will do if you start telling people your lies about me." His mood had quickly turned to anger, and she felt her blood grow cold as he stared her down with his piercing black eyes.

"Your threats mean nothing to me," Ludie said, stepping to the side to avoid him. She stepped off the sidewalk and crossed the street toward the courthouse, and this time he didn't follow her. A wave of panic surged through her when she heard him shout across the street to her. His words would have been misinterpreted by anyone who heard, and that fact scared her almost more than what he said.

"I promise, Sweetheart. You have my

word!" He shouted cheerfully across the street. *I promise I will hurt you if you tell!* he was really saying. She turned and looked back at him and he gave a quick wave, then turned and walked away.

Ludie cut across the courthouse lawn and headed straight for Brynn's shop. She walked in to find her finishing up on some orders. The scent in the shop was clean, fresh, and light, in deep contrast to her dark, swirling emotions.

"What's wrong, honey?" Brynn asked when she looked up to see her expression. "You look like you've just seen a ghost," she told her.

"I wish." Ludie felt the adrenaline that had just coursed through her settle down, leaving her suddenly fatigued.

Brynn pulled out a folding chair and told her to sit down. "Talk to me." Ludie hesitated, looking back at the front door of the shop to ensure no one was there.

"It's just us," Brynn said. Ludie shuddered and seemed unsure. "I promise. The back door is locked and bolted. Dear God," she breathed, "what is wrong?"

Ludie drew in a sharp breath and told her what he'd said. Brynn's facial expression quickly went from concerned to angry. "He won't get away with this. You've got to call the police."

"No. This town is too small. He won't take kindly to their threats, and he could make life very difficult for me. I don't want Poppa, Birdie or Mavis to find out about any of this."

"I think it's sweet of you to consider their

feelings, but your safety is a bit more important, and I know they would agree with me. I'm calling Roxy."

Despite Ludie's protest, Brynn dug her phone out from under a pile of wicking supplies and touched the screen to bring up the number. It went straight to voicemail, and she left a message.

"Go to the back, sit at my desk and read, or just rest for a while," Brynn ordered. "Let me think about this."

"Fine, but just for now," she agreed. "I can't hide forever you know."

"I know," Brynn smiled. "That's why I called Roxy."

An hour later, Roxy arrived and Brynn told her what Eric had said and done.

"Oh, no he won't," she responded, slamming her fist down on the counter. "A bloke like that's full of hot air," she said. "He's all talk, and not man enough to take action." Brynn agreed, adding that he was a coward and only had the confidence to confront someone alone, someone smaller and weaker than him.

Ludie tried to relax and take comfort in her friends' words. She'd been surprised to find out that his business had actually suffered, realizing that Roxy was a woman of her word. Whatever the hold she had on the men she met, it worked. Poor Dennis, he didn't know what he was getting himself into when Roxy agreed to go out with him. Ludie was ashamed to admit to herself that she enjoyed the benefits of friendship with someone so strong having her back.

"Besides, if he even thinks of putting a hand on you, Ben will make him wish he'd never even come to this town."

"What? You told Ben?" Ludie was angry at first, but then calmed down when Brynn told her he had asked almost every day how she was doing and if Eric had shown his face. She was touched that he cared. The day of her miscarriage, she had thought he merely pitied her and was being kind because she was Brynn's friend.

"You don't get it, do you?" Brynn said, exchanging a knowing look with Roxy. Ludie frowned, sending her friends the signal that she didn't want to discuss this anymore. On the inside, however, she was smiling and had a warm feeling all the way to her core. Ben really cared about her.

The next evening she was at the farmhouse with Poppa. He seemed so happy to have her back home and took every opportunity to let her know. If he wasn't complaining about how he had to buy milk in the small bottles and bread in the small loaves when it was just him, he was talking about how the house was just too quiet without her constant chattering. It was Poppa's way of letting her know he loved her. He wanted her there, and knowing that fact truly warmed her heart.

"What is your schedule for the week?" he asked her.

"Oh," she said. "I meant to write it on the

calendar. I'm doing the breakfast and lunch shifts at Birdie's and afternoons at the candle shop." She took the calendar off its hook on the kitchen wall and began penciling her hours in the appropriate spots.

"I'll be here at the house most all this week," he offered. "But I'm driving to Houston with Birdie day after tomorrow to pick up some things at the restaurant supply house."

At this, Ludie raised an eyebrow in question. "You sure are spending a lot of time with Birdie lately," she smiled. "What's up with that?"

"What's up? What's *up* with that? What's all this gangster talk?" He mocked her in an effort to change the subject. It didn't work.

"I just notice she's been out here a few times lately and I've seen you at the café more than usual." She hung the calendar back on its hook and sat down across from him.

"Well you might remember, it's been hard to plan meals with it just being me," he said, shifting the blame to Ludie. "Sometimes it's easier just to grab a bite at Ladybirds and, besides, Birdie has been kind enough to cook for me a couple of times. I like those casseroles she makes."

Ludie smiled at his response. Birdie and Nanny had been close friends for years and she was a friend of the family. It seemed almost a natural progression that she and Poppa would grow closer. Suppressing a twinge of feeling disloyal to her Nanny, she told herself this was good for both of them.

"Casseroles, huh?" she laughed, tossing a towel at him.

On the evening of the day Poppa and Birdie went to Houston, Ludie came home from work knowing her grandfather wouldn't be home until much later. When she pulled her truck into the drive she felt a strange sense of foreboding. A slight shiver ran down her spine and she chided herself for being so ridiculous. She could handle being at home alone.

Walking up the steps, she shifted her bag and the day's mail she'd gotten on the way in and opened the door. They rarely felt the need to lock the doors as the nearest neighbor was nearly a half mile away. Throwing the mail down on the table, she took the steps two at a time and went to her room. She felt the hair stand up on the back of her neck when she saw her bed, neatly made. She never made her bed. Although she'd always kept a fairly neat bedroom, it had always seemed unnecessary to make a bed you were just going to climb back into. Maybe Poppa had made it, she reasoned. No, he never had before. Why would he start now? Just being happy to have her home wasn't likely to cause him to change his habits like that. He'd always respected her privacy. Perhaps he was just trying to welcome her home. He must have made the bed as a way of letting her know he was happy she was back home in her old room. She forced a smile.

Taking a step back, she reached over and

opened the closet door, cautiously. Her clothes were completely rearranged, hung by color and in perfect order, two fingers' width between each hanger. *Just like Eric's closet.* She suppressed another shiver and backed up, turning to run back down the stairs. She locked and bolted both the front door and the back and closed all the blinds. She dared to peek out the front door, opening it slightly and calling for the dog. He didn't answer, and that alone was unusual. Typically he waited for Ludie in the drive when he heard her truck crunching on the gravel of the long driveway.

The phone rang, startling her further. It was Poppa.

"We're gonna' be later than usual, Mouse. We had to go clear across to the other side of town to get some of the things Birdie needs. It'll be long after dark, so don't wait up for me if you get tired."

"Okay," she answered weakly. "Y'all be careful."

"What's wrong?" he asked, suddenly sounding worried.

"Oh, no… nothing's wrong. I'm just tired." They spoke briefly and hung up. Looking around her, the farm house seemed suddenly so dark and quiet. She knew Eric had been in the house and it frightened her. She went into the kitchen and made some coffee. She knew she wouldn't sleep before Poppa came home.

Opening the refrigerator and removing her vanilla creamer, she tried again to dismiss her concerns. Eric was just trying to scare her and she wasn't going to give him the satisfaction.

Inhaling the aroma of the fresh brew she took a cup from the cabinet and poured herself some coffee. She shook the creamer bottle gently, flipped open the top, and poured it into her cup. Swirling it gently with a spoon, she felt herself becoming riled at Eric's audacity. Whatever message he was trying to send her he was going about it the wrong way. She could call the police, she reasoned. But then what? It would only serve to anger him more.

It wasn't as late as she had feared when Poppa finally came home. He had driven straight home after taking Birdie to her house, and seemed surprised to find her sitting in the living room drinking coffee. The TV was off and the house was quiet.

"Ludie, why are you up so late? Tired as you are working two jobs," he grumbled, "you ought to be sleeping."

"Oh, no, Poppa, I'm fine. I decided to wait up and do some reading."

He looked around her, and found no reading material within arms' length.

"Talk to me," he said. "You're afraid, and I don't like it. Is Eric doing anything to upset you?" For just a brief moment, she considered telling him, but that would mean telling him about her pregnancy and she just couldn't bear the thought of bringing him so much pain.

"I guess I'm just still taking it hard." Getting up from the chair she went over to him and kissed him good night. "Now that you're home, I'm much more relaxed. I'm going to bed. I love you."

His eyes followed her as she made her way up the stairs, concerned about her and angry with the fool who'd made her so upset.

She tossed and turned in her bed until nearly three a.m. She couldn't quite shake the feeling she was being watched. He'd been in her room, and she knew it. She felt even more violated than she had when he'd hurt her.

When her alarm finally went off in the morning, she realized she must have finally given in to sleep.

She got up and stepped into the shower, letting the hot water run over her while she wept. *It isn't fair*, she raged inside. *Who does he think he is?*

# Chapter 13

When Ludie got to the café she found the busy morning kept her mind occupied. Falling into the familiar rhythm, she was able to shake her thoughts of Eric for a few minutes at a time. Still wounded by his rejection, she vacillated between loving him and fearing him. Each time he invaded her thoughts again, she threw herself further into her routine and into being attentive to her customers. The good old boys' network was quite happy with their new booth since the re-opening. That was one thing she could credit Eric with: his design had allowed for a large, round table-booth, right in the middle of the diner where they would be the center of all the activity. *Eric,* she thought, disgusted that he'd crossed her mind again.

Ludie focused her attention on the men and their conversation. She found it strangely comforting. As she filled their cups, she found herself amused by their topics of conversation. Before long it had turned to unemployment.

"Hey Owen," Melvin said. "Did your boy ever get a job?"

"Hell no," the old fire chief replied angrily, and geared himself up for a debate. "He's been doing construction jobs in this town for years, and now he can't get a lick of work because all those illegal aliens are taking the jobs." There were a few nods of agreement around the table.

"I know what you mean," said one of the men. "It ain't so bad if they're here legally, it's the ones that are here under the radar that makes me so mad."

"Yea, well we're not supposed to be calling 'em illegal aliens," said Owen, "even though that's what they are." He unrolled the napkin that held his silverware. "Us calling them 'undocumented workers' is just a lie. A politically correct lie. That's like calling drug dealers 'unlicensed pharmacists'." Laughter surrounded the table, although this was a subject the men took very seriously.

"I think it's these new contractors coming in from the city," one of the men said. "They just want to hire these poor illegals for pennies and then experienced people like Owen's boy have to do without work. "

"That's right," answered Owen. "And my boy pays his taxes. You think those workers pay any taxes? If they do, I'd like to see proof of it." Realizing Ludie was back at the table, they quickly hushed their conversation, knowing it was obvious the contractor they spoke of was Eric.

"It's okay," she told them, and they looked up at her in contrived confusion. "I know you're talking about Eric and you're right. Don't ease up on him to spare my feelings. We're not together anymore." The men didn't even make an effort to appear disappointed in their break-up. Owen told Ludie he was awfully sorry, and then the men went right on with their conversation. She shook her head as she walked away. The men in small Texas towns like Blackwater had been bitter about immigration issues as long as she could remember.

"Did you see that job they got goin' over off County Line road?" one of them asked. "Illegals. 'Ever last one of 'em." Ludie went to the kitchen, strangely satisfied that others saw Eric for what he was. *What was I thinking?* she wondered. *He was all wrong for me and I was blind not to see him for what he was.*

She was pleasantly surprised that Tyler and Courtney had picked up on the diner routine more quickly than she had expected. By the time the lunch crowd was starting to thin out, she left them both in Mavis's capable hands. She seemed to have regained her strength and was more than capable of running the dining room while Birdie stayed on top of Robert in the kitchen. They were receiving a shipment in the back at the moment.

Ludie hung up her apron and made her way down the sidewalk to the candle shop. She was happy to find Ben there and somewhat amused to find him standing in a puddle of wax. Fighting back a giggle, she went to help him.

"Let me guess," she said. "Brynn's doing a clinical rotation and you've been completely overwhelmed by orders."

Looking down at his wax-splotched clothes, he gave her a sheepish grin. "You got it, kid! Now quit laughing and help me out here."

She grabbed a couple of wide putty knives and handed him one. The two of them began scraping up the hardening wax and cleaning up the mess. When they'd cleaned up, she helped him with the orders. They worked well together and accomplished a great deal by late afternoon.

Chimes alerted them to the front door, and Katherine walked in, complete with her smug, self-satisfied grin. She seemed to draw great satisfaction from flaunting her relationship with Eric and wasted no time in bringing him up, in a round-about way. "I need something romantic," she purred. "Preferably aromatherapy. Don't you have something herbal, something sensual?" She tapped a manicured nail on her red pouty lips. I hear they have fragrances for every mood. Maybe even something a little exotic," she laughed. "I'm having company tonight and I want to set the mood." An expression of satisfaction flashed in her eyes.

Clenching her teeth, determined not to let Katherine get the best of her, Ludie showed her where the herbal scents were located. Ben brushed past her and scooped a votive off the shelf, waving it in front of Katherine's face. Ludie resisted the urge to strangle him.

"This is patchouli," he said. "It's a known aphrodisiac. Would you believe patchouli was discovered by ancient Indian medicine men? They encouraged the villagers to dab a little of the oil on their bodies to encourage warmth and openness within the tribe." Katherine was leaning forward, hanging on his every word. "True story," Ben continued, his eyes squinted in mock seriousness. "Only problem was, the people got

156

carried away. They didn't just dab a little on, they rubbed their bodies down with it. Can you just picture that?" He simulated the action by rubbing his hands all over his chest and abdomen. "All that heated oil rubbed all over their naked bodies? It increased openness and warmth so *much*, in fact, that there was a documented population boom that year."

Katherine pursed her lips, focusing intently on his story.

"Oh don't worry, darling, if one of these little magic candles doesn't do the trick, we guarantee 'em." He tossed a votive in the air and caught it in his other hand with a smack. "You just march right back in here tomorrow and tell us it didn't get you laid and you'll get back every dime. You can use the refund money down at the pharmacy towards that little blue pill they make."

Ludie choked back a laugh, excusing herself, and quickly stepped to the back of the shop.

Katherine made an attempt to maintain her dignity and, after being somehow unable to find the right scent, she left the shop. Ben turned and looked at Ludie, his eyebrows moving up and down rapidly. She giggled in response and threw a tea light at him. He flashed a guilty grin and a tiny glow of warmth began in her belly and spread outward. He could always make her smile.

After work, Ludie stopped by Roxy's house. She found her friend sitting in a lounge chair furiously scrawling addresses onto envelopes. "What on earth are you doing?" Ludie asked her.

"There's nothing wrong with ordering a few catalogues every now and then, is there?" she asked, pointing to a stack of magazines on the coffee table. Ludie picked one up and starting flipping through it.

"Oh my gosh!" she said, "You're ordering junk mail! This is Eric's address!"

Roxy laughed. "The ones at the backs of the magazines are the best. 'Satisfy your woman. Male enhancement. Exploring your feminine side.' It never hurts to have a little advice from time to time."

It would seem that Roxy and Ben were in cahoots. Either that or they both got a kick out of attacking Eric's masculinity. Roxy gave a wicked laugh, and then noticed Ludie's serious expression.

Ludie said she had something important to discuss and made Roxy promise to behave, no matter what she told her. She also made her promise to remain calm, and then told her about her suspicions that Eric had gone into the farmhouse the night before.

"Suspicions? *Suspicions?*" Roxy shouted. "You know good and well he was in there. It couldn't have been anyone else! Suspicions, my bloody arse!" The redhead was on her feet, pacing furiously. "The bastard won't get away with this," she muttered, and went on a verbal tirade, seemingly unaware of Ludie's continued presence. She stopped, pulling in a deep breath.

"Let's take a walk, why don't we?" Roxy

suggested, apparently calmer after taking more deep breaths. "It'll do you some good." Ludie reluctantly agreed and the two walked down the block and around the corner.

It was a nice night, although a bit cool. Roxy mentioned Dennis.

"You mean the volunteer firefighter, Dennis?" Ludie asked. "What's the story?"

"We've gone out a few times. Oh darling," Roxy purred. "He's gorgeous!" She gave her a conspiratorial wink. "Delicious."

Ludie was ecstatic for her friend. Dennis was such a small-town laid back kind of guy, and Roxy was, well, *Roxy*. She couldn't believe she hadn't seen this coming. What a great match!

Ludie drew her hands up into her loose sweater sleeves for warmth, and stepped up a bit to keep up with Roxy's hurried pace. "Slow down," she told her. "I thought this was going to be a nice relaxing stroll. Not a marathon."

"You're right, Luv." Roxy slowed her pace and smiled. "I'll slow down. This walk is already helping your mood. You just wait. It does me a world of good to see you smile." It was a beautiful night, Ludie had to admit.

"I hope you're not intentionally baiting Eric," Ludie said.

Roxy's eyebrows lifted in mock surprise, her fingers pointing to her chest. "Me? Oh, no, you've got me all wrong, mate. It's just a bloody walk. I doubt we'll even run into him." She pursed her lips, obviously pleased with herself about something.

Ludie began to doubt her friend's word when they just happened to turn the corner off the main square and past Eric's apartment. As soon as Ludie saw Eric's car, she was at first shocked, then shortly overtaken by a wave of giggles.

"How long do you think it'll take him to find it?" Roxy asked. On the back of Eric's sleek, black sports car was a colorful bumper sticker placed indiscreetly on the rear bumper. On a rainbow background it read in bold print, "Proud of who I am." Stepping up their pace, the two sprinted past, assaulted with a fresh burst of giggles. A gay pride sticker. Knowing Eric and how he felt about certain things, Ludie knew this would be a horrific humiliation to him. Good for him.

"You didn't!" Ludie squealed, short of breath.

"Oh I did, darling. I did."

# Chapter 14

After the incident at the farmhouse, Ludie didn't see or hear from Eric for a few days. On all fronts it appeared that he'd gotten the message and moved on with his life, no longer focused on her. The following Monday, however, she saw him when he came into the café for coffee with a client.

He had the audacity to walk right in the front door, evidently convinced that she'd not told anyone about her pregnancy or the events that had transpired between them. He gave her a smug, self-satisfied smile when he walked in, and took a seat. Her heart fluttered wildly in her chest at the sight of him. Birdie paid him no mind and, if it hadn't been for Courtney, he probably wouldn't even have been given a menu or a cup of coffee.

When Ludie looked up to see Courtney standing at Eric's booth, smiling and flirting, she knew the girl wasn't to blame. She was young, and didn't have any idea about Ludie's relationship with him. All she knew, apparently, was that this very nice-looking, charming man was paying her attention. She didn't seem concerned that he was older than her and besides, Ludie reasoned, she was probably just working on a good tip. Ignoring the ridiculous display Eric was putting on and going to the back,

Ludie offered to help Robert with some cooking, something she'd never bothered to do before. He seemed surprised, almost flattered, then immediately reminded her that it was his kitchen and that Birdie actually had very little say about what went on in there. He was a bit territorial, Ludie remembered. Birdie promptly noticed the conversation and, more importantly, she peeped out to the dining room and noticed the reason Ludie had suddenly decided to take up cooking. She gave Ludie a crooked little smile and told her to go down to the candle shop and help out there. "It's a little slow here," she told her, much to Robert's dismay. "Now go," Birdie told her. "Use the back door."

Oh, how Ludie loved her boss. Birdie never ceased to amaze her with her ability to read people and, as Ludie walked down the alley behind the row of shops, she wondered just how much Birdie really knew. She was a very intuitive woman and seemed to love Ludie as if she were her very own grandchild. All the more reason to make sure she never found out. If Birdie knew, then surely Poppa would know, too. The two had become even closer as of late, and it seemed there were no secrets between them. What one knew, the other one was soon to find out. Ludie resolved to never let that happen, and made her way to the candle shop, surprising Brynn by her appearance through the back door.

Later on that very same night on the outskirts of town, Eric lay in Katherine's bed, watching her undress. He admired the soft curves of her body, and thought of the long night that stretched out before them. "C'mere," he murmured in a sultry voice.

"Just a minute," she laughed. "There's something I need to do." She disappeared into her newly-refurbished master bath, closing the door gently behind her. Smiling at his earlier decision to install French doors, he got up and padded across the carpet to spy. Her back was to him and all he could see was her rifling through a drawer. When she drew back her hand with a tube of cream, he ducked back to avoid being spotted. *Spermicidal foam.* He raced to the bed and had just struck his previous pose when she opened the doors and reappeared before him.

"What were you doing?" he asked.

"Ah, nothing to concern yourself with," she smiled. "Just a little insurance."

"Insurance? What are you talking about?" His brows drew together and his eyes turned dark.

"I was just thinking," she said, "lately, I mean. Sex is a recreational activity, but it doesn't have to be a procreational one." She tossed her head back and laughed. "We don't need any documented changes in population," she said, explaining further. His dark eyes narrowed with confusion as she continued. "I don't want to get pregnant. I'm finished with all that."

"Haven't you even thought of it?" he asked. "Even a little?" He knew she was older, but she had money. *A lot of money*, he thought. And he wasn't getting any younger either. Maybe he had just missed his one and only opportunity to pass on his strong good looks, and his good name. Any son would be fortunate to be born to a man like him.

"No," she said matter-of-factly, shaking him from his reverie. "I have no desire to be tied down with a child. Or to *anyone*, for that matter. My husband understands that, why can't you?" She licked her full, sensual lips, fully intent on continuing with their evening together.

He studied her for signs of softness, for any maternal instinct, and saw her perhaps for the very first time for what she was. The very qualities that had drawn him to her were now liabilities. She was a woman in control and he wasn't the kind of man to relinquish control to anyone, especially a woman.

First, Ludie had told him she was going to be a mother, whether he liked it or not. Now, Katherine was telling him she would not be, giving him no consideration in the decision. Feeling anger rising in him from his perceived loss of control, he simultaneously felt his desire dwindling. With that, he threw back the high-thread count Egyptian sheets and the satin duvet cover and jumped to his feet. Katherine looked at him for a moment, her thin brow arched in question.

"I have something to do," he told her, and his voice was completely devoid of emotion. What he felt was so beyond emotion. It was a mission, a stronger determination than he'd ever known himself to feel.

Moments later he was in his car on the way back into town, taking the curves at ninety miles per hour, his fist clenched on the steering wheel, his jaw set in determination. His steely resolve was like a rock within him and he drew a perverse thrill at the possibilities ahead. A woman as powerful as Katherine may call the shots in her own life, he thought, but a weak child like Ludie would not control his.

The following morning Roxy showed up at the candle shop with a box full of black tee-shirts and ball caps. She immediately began unfolding the shirts to check sizes, handing them out as if this were business as usual. Ludie and Brynn, along with Ben, who was helping at the shop today, stopped what they were doing to examine the shirts and hats. They were each emblazoned with the initials "INS" and caused a curious reaction from the group.

"What on earth?" asked Brynn. "What are these for?" Roxy laughed and informed the group that they'd be visiting the work site of Eric's construction crew this afternoon. Eric, it seemed, would be simultaneously occupied in Houston for the day, although Ludie couldn't imagine how Roxy had ascertained that information. She didn't even ask.

The afternoon proved to be more than entertaining. They arrived in Ben's SUV to find a work crew in place in a new development off county line road. The crew had littered the street in front of the huge homes with construction debris and the men were currently taking a break under the shade of a big oak tree. The sound of Tejano music blared from the speakers of a work van in the yard, much to the upset of the neighbors, judging by the expressions on the faces of a young couple standing across the street.

"What are we supposed to do?" Ludie asked from the backseat. "When we get out, I mean." She leaned forward to look out the front window as Ben brought the vehicle to a halt.

"Nothing," laughed Roxy. "Nothing at all. All we have to do is get out and walk toward them. The rest will take care of itself." Ben and Brynn exchanged glances, and they all burst into laughter.

Forcing a more serious expression, Roxy got out a clipboard with some typed papers on it. For all Ludie knew it could have been her unfolded electrical bill but it sent a message that it was most likely very important government documents. They opened the doors, each stepping out at the same time, tee-shirts and ball caps in place, fully emblazoned with INS. As they took a few steps, the first worker to notice them alerted the others, and they took off running. They reached their dilapidated cars and the van with the loud speakers in a matter of seconds, piled in and sped off.

"That, my friends," said Roxy, through gales of laughter, "is how it's done."

"Nooo," Ludie said, once realization had sunk in. "Those poor guys!"

"Oh, poor guys, nothing." Roxy pursed her

lips. "They are here illegally. If I had really wanted to be mean, I'd have called the real INS. They'd not only be losing this particular job, but would also be likely facing deportation."

Ludie thought about it for a moment. It was hurting Eric more than anyone. "Besides," she added, in hopes of easing her own guilt, "Owen's son and all his workers are legal citizens and they haven't been able to get work."

She didn't feel terribly great about it, but considering the fact that Roxy was involved, she reasoned it could be much worse.

# Chapter 15

That afternoon Eric pressed the buttons on his phone for the third time in as many minutes. He held it up to his ear, waiting for it to ring at the other end. Finally someone answered and spoke.

"Where is the crew?" Eric asked. He paused, growing more furious as he listened to the voice on the other end.

"What? I don't care. Find them." He ended the call and pocketed his phone. This was not turning out to be a good day. Apparently the work crews from three new homes had abandoned their jobs without notice and were now unreachable. He had deadlines, for heaven's sake, and delays like this didn't help. On considering deadlines, his thoughts turned to Ludie. It wasn't going to be *her* day, either.

When Ludie and the others had returned to the shop, they quickly changed clothes and hid away their shirts and ball caps. They immersed themselves in candle-making and did a very good job of looking innocent of any mischievous activity, just in case they had any customers. They didn't want word to leak out that the visit from the immigration authorities had anything to do with them.

The next day Ludie went straight to the shop from the Ladybird Café and was surprised to see Roxy in the back with Brynn. She just barely caught a glimpse of them hiding something and exchanging a wary glance. One thing she'd learned was to be able to tell when those two were up to something, so she asked.

They were too quick to answer. "Oh, nothing, no worries" answered Roxy at the same time Brynn was saying, "Just work stuff."

Ludie casually made her way to the work table where they were standing and then quickly reached the spot where she'd seen Brynn stashing something. She picked up a beautiful sterling silver key chain, a key with a BMW logo attached. There was a tiny engraving on the back with a message.

*If found, please return to Eric Butler. Large cash reward.* His address was listed just beneath the message.

Realization dawned and she looked up at Roxy, knowing she was the instigator. "What is this about?" she demanded, her hand on her hip for emphasis. "Eric doesn't drive a Beamer."

Roxy told her it would be a shame if this valuable key chain just happened to be dropped on the sidewalk in the worst part of town. Ludie threw her hands in the air. "You're ridiculous! I'm going on the record to say I want no part of this." But her inner voice said she wished *she* had thought of it first.

Two evenings later, Eric was sitting in his apartment sipping on a glass of one of his favorite vintage wines and listening to the soothing sounds of jazz. He heard footsteps on the stairs and went to the door to glance through the peephole, daring to hope it would be Ludie on the other side, having come to her senses.

He was surprised to see a large black man with a gold tooth and designs razor-cut into the side of his hair. He was accompanied by a rough-looking white man aged, weathered, and embellished with piercings and prison tattoos. They both wore determined expressions on their faces.

"What do you need?" Eric shouted through the door once the men had knocked. "You've got the wrong address, Buddy."

"I got something for you," the man said. "Now open the door and give me my reward," he demanded. Eric was horrified at the mere suggestion he would even consider exchanging money for drugs with a common street dealer. He attached the chain on the door and opened it a crack. The man told him, "Open the door and give me my damn money!"

"I have no money for you and I will not do business with a criminal." He pushed the door closed but before he could lock it he felt it give way beneath the pressure of one of the man's size thirteen feet. The door flung open. Before Eric could defend himself, he felt the man's fist connect with his jaw and saw his blood splattering, hitting the door and landing on his throw rug. The other man dropped some sort of key ring onto his chest.

When he regained consciousness later, he saw that his DVD player and TV were gone. His

170

wallet had been on the bar near his phone, and both items were missing as well. He was shocked that such activity could even occur in such a small town, and went to the freezer for crushed ice. Wrapping it in a towel and applying it to his swollen eye and cheek, he shook his head in dismay, realizing he would need to invest in a security system and perhaps another weapon. A fine lot of good a gun does, he thought, if it's not within your reach at all times.

The next few weeks were fairly uneventful, and Ludie had easily settled back into her life at the farmhouse with Poppa. There were no further signs of any presence of Eric, and she was glad. Feeling certain that he had gotten the message her delightfully vengeful friends had sent, she began to feel more comfortable coming and going, and found herself looking over her shoulder less and less.

She spent more time at the candle shop, comfortable that Mavis was regaining her strength and was of great help to Birdie. Even Tyler and Courtney were picking up their pace and growing more confident in their skills. Brynn's business was thriving, and she was needed at the shop more often to keep up with the orders. In the middle of March, Ben had made the decision to leave the refinery to help manage the shop full time. Brynn was delighted, as her heart was leading her into a full-time career as a nurse. She loved the candles, but there was something so incredibly rewarding about nursing and it was a battle she fought within herself before making the decision to let Ben take over. She had been afraid to reveal her news to her brother and was relieved when he'd responded so eagerly. She would've been required to hire someone to manage the shop if he hadn't agreed to take over. She would still help at the shop, of course, but had made the commitment to extend her studies and wind up in a full-time position with the hospital. Ludie made herself available at the shop for extended hours to ease the transition. Ben was proving more than capable and she delighted in watching him deal with suppliers and customers. She knew that part of his devotion to the business was out of a desire to provide for his nephew's future. Blake was lucky to have him.

In time, Ludie became more and more proficient at chandlery, the art of candlemaking, as well as assembling beautiful and elegant gift baskets. She loved making aromatherapy products and bath soaps and lotions. They made for a wonderful compliment to the line of candles and were a hit with the customers. She and Ben worked well together, a fact that wasn't lost on either Brynn or Roxy. Both of them had commented on seeing the two huddled together in the shop, discussing an order or new fragrances.

Blake still came to the shop every day after school, and seemed to truly enjoy the time he spent with his uncle. They shared an easy relationship, and Brynn loved that her son respected her brother so well. It wasn't the same as having his father in his life, but having such a strong male role model was a significant factor.

He was excelling in his school work, and made his mother proud.

One afternoon when they were working, Ludie asked Ben what time he was leaving to pick up Blake from school. He told her that Brynn didn't have a rotation that day and she had picked him up herself. It was quiet in the shop after that, without Blake's loud laughter and the sounds of his electronic games. Ben told Ludie there was something important he wanted to discuss with her, and she put down the jars she'd been labeling to pay attention. He had a very serious look on his face, and seemed to be hesitating, as if struggling to form the words. *Oh no,* she thought, *he doesn't need my help anymore.* Business was steady, but not as busy as it had been during the holidays, of course. She was heartsick at the notion of not being there every day, but had to admit he'd become a strong business manager. If he needed to scale down a bit, she would certainly understand.

Their impending conversation was delayed when the phone rang. Ludie answered it, and heard Birdie crying on the other end of the line. She was unable to make sense of her words. She hung up the phone, and raced for the door. Turning to look back at Ben, she shouted, "I'm sorry, I have to go!" He saw the color drain from her face and he quickly began turning off the melting pots, locking the door behind him as he left the shop. He had seen her race down the sidewalk toward Birdie's and made hasty work of following her. He arrived to see Birdie with her hands on either of Ludie's shoulders, looking her in the eye. Fortunately there were no customers as they had thinned out after lunch. Birdie had apparently stayed to clean up and take inventory, as there were several supply forms on a clipboard on the counter.

He saw Ludie bring her hands to her face, bursting into tears. "It's all happening so fast," he heard Birdie say. "We never saw it coming. She never let on."

He raced to Ludie's side, dreading the news. "It's Mavis!" she cried. "She's had a recurrence of her cancer, and she's in the hospital. She never told anyone!" She sobbed between words, struggling to explain to him what she'd just been told. "They have her on hospice services," she said. "I didn't know it could happen this fast. They're not giving her very long."

Birdie was turning off lights, and reached for her purse and keys. "We need to go now," she said. Ben offered to drive them.

"You're neither one in any shape to drive. I'll get my car." He wouldn't take no for an answer, Ludie knew.

By the time the two women had locked up the café, Ben was pulling up in front in his SUV. When they arrived at the hospital, they made their way to the hospice floor. Upon finding Mavis's room, they saw Melvin sitting next to her, holding her hand. None of them were surprised, as Melvin had been by her side every step of the way. Mavis had truly grown to love him in return, and thanked God every day for his devotion to her.

Melvin looked up when they walked in, and Ludie thought she'd never seen such a sad, lost look on anyone's face since she and Poppa had lost Nanny. A single tear rolled down Melvin's cheek and he looked back down at Mavis, as if he couldn't bear to take his eyes off her for even a moment out of his fear of losing her.

"What happened?" asked Birdie. "I thought she was better. She beat the cancer. What happened?" she repeated in a small, frightened voice.

"She *was* better," Melvin answered. "I heard the doctor tell her when she finished her radiation that the cancer was undetectable." He looked down at his hand that held Mavis's fragile one so tenderly. "He told her to keep up with her appointments and have the scans to make sure it didn't come back. But it did come back," he said. "And she never told me. Not until yesterday, anyway," he finished. "Thing is, she told me it was back like it was no big deal. She figured she could fight it and win again."

"Her little dog," he said, his eyes filling with tears again, "she made me promise to take care of her." He laughed, almost bitterly. "Can you see me with that tiny little rat she calls a dog? It's too little to even hardly see at the other end of the leash. I'll be out in my yard yelling, 'Bitsy, come on Bitsy,' and none of the neighbors will know who I'm talking to. She loves that dog," he said, choking back a sob.

This time he was unable to suppress it, and sobbed more freely. "I should've known," he cried. "I should've seen she was getting weaker." He was shaking his head sadly.

"No, you couldn't have known," Birdie said, crossing the room to put her hand on his shoulder and pat him. "I didn't see it either. When she took the past few days off work, she said it was because she had some things to take care of. I never suspected it had come back." Birdie, too, looked as if she would cry at any moment. "She told me it was time to turn the dining room over to Tyler and Courtney for a while and see how they did." She laughed through her tears, adding, "She told me she'd done her best with them and it was time to turn them loose. Said she was looking to retire soon and have some time to herself. I had no idea this was happening!" Birdie looked down, pacing furiously.

Ben had taken Ludie's hand in his, rubbing the back of her hand with his fingers, soothing her as she sniffed back tears. "What are they saying?" she asked Melvin in a whisper. "The doctors, I mean." He looked up, but found it hard to make eye contact. He got up and stepped to the doorway, motioning for the others to step out into the hallway so they could speak freely.

"They're saying it's not long. When I brought her in this morning she was feeling pretty weak. She could barely walk, so I held her and walked her in, but they brought a wheelchair when they saw she was having so much trouble."

He relayed the day's events to them, telling them she'd had a scan which revealed metastasis, meaning the cancer had spread to other areas, like her lungs and bones. They'd told him that it was too late for any further chemotherapy to be successful and recommended hospice care as the best alternative. Mavis, weak as she was, had agreed to it and had been immediately admitted.

"They put in an IV," Melvin continued. "They've been putting some morphine in it to keep her comfortable. That's why she's been sleeping so much. They did say they were going to take the IV out and give her liquid medicine under her tongue."

"How long?" Ludie whispered, choking back her tears. "How much time does she have?"

"Not long," he answered. "They won't give me a time, not even an estimate. They said sometimes people can go days and days without food or water. Part of the reason she knew something was wrong was because she couldn't swallow anymore." A single tear traced its way down his face and he didn't bother to wipe it away this time.

He went on to explain that Mavis had made her wishes clear. She didn't want antibiotics or extended IV fluids or a feeding tube. She didn't want any kind of heroics, only comfort measures. She had agreed to pain medications and they were giving them to her as she needed them, as often as every hour. She'd made the decisions for her advance directives when she'd first been diagnosed several months ago, and confirmed this morning that those were still her wishes.

"She's been sleeping ever since we first got here," he said, sadly.

Ludie reached out to Birdie, laying her head on her shoulder, and sobbed.

"I know, honey," Birdie said softly. "I know."

"Someone should call Poppa," Ludie said suddenly. Birdie agreed to make the phone call, and Ludie asked Melvin to excuse her for a moment. She and Ben walked down the hall to a quiet, softly-lit waiting room, where he held her and she wept. He was such a comfort to her. It had completely left her mind that Ben had wanted to speak with her about something important and it no longer occurred to her to be concerned about her job. All she could think of was Mavis and how quickly she'd taken such a turn for the worst.

Poppa came to the hospital right away after Birdie called him. Ludie noticed what a strong source of comfort he was to Birdie and she was glad he was there. They had all been at her bedside for over an hour when Mavis woke up. She opened her eyes weakly, and seemed surprised to see them all there.

"Well," she whispered, "I guess I know how to draw a crowd." She gave a soft laugh. "Did Melvin tell you what the doctors said?" She fiddled with the blanket, rolling and twirling the edges of it. She avoided eye contact.

It was Birdie who spoke up first. "They don't know everything," she said. "You're strong. And besides," she continued, "you were so busy and active, running my dining room just a few days ago." She stopped at that, her eyes clouding

178

over with tears. "You were pretty near running *me*," she added.

"I've already come to terms with this," Mavis said. "I made my decisions months ago, and nothing's changed. I didn't expect to have this extra time, but I did. And it's been a gift." She looked over at Melvin, who was sitting next to her with his hand on the bed next to her. She placed her hand on top of his. "I'm so grateful for the time I've had. But I'm at peace with this. I'm ready for whatever happens next." She smiled, and it occurred to Ludie that she really did seem at peace. Mavis had always seemed to be strong in her faith, and spiritually secure. Ludie found comfort in that. She went closer to the bed and pulled a chair up to the side of it. She lowered the rail and leaned over, kissing Mavis softly on the cheek. "I love you," she whispered.

"I love you, too, Sugar," she said quietly, "and everything's okay. You'll see. Everything happens for a reason. I don't know what God has in mind, but I know that as long as we trust Him, we'll be all right." She looked Ludie square in the eye and smiled, taking her hand and squeezing it, turning it over to kiss the back of it.

Birdie occupied herself straightening the room, emptying cups and a napkin off the bedside table. She looked around the room and made sure there was nothing else to be done. She always needed to be in control, Ludie thought, but this time there was no way she *could* be. Mavis was her dearest friend.

"We need to go," Birdie told the others.

"She needs to get some rest and she can't very well do that with us here yappin' in her ears, now can she?" She started fidgeting for her purse, and Ludie looked back at Mavis, who smiled and gave her a quick wink. Birdie leaned over and gave Mavis a kiss and then instructed Melvin to call if there were any changes or if she needed anything.

Mavis reassured them all that Melvin had gotten everything she needed from her house and that he'd even called her nephew for her. He was planning on driving in from Houston in the evening when he got off work.

When Ben pulled his vehicle up in front of the café, Birdie thanked him profusely as she got out.

"My pleasure," he answered. "If you need anything at all, you call me." The sunlight reflected on the thick, golden waves of his short hair. His smile and his offer were genuine, and Ludie was grateful. She went back to the shop with him and helped him make sure they'd closed everything out for the day properly. They'd left so quickly before that it hadn't occurred to either of them to close out the cash register or lock the safe, so they took the opportunity to do so then. She gathered her purse and keys, and thanked him for being so helpful. He smiled warmly and told her he considered it an honor to be included in these sacred and very personal moments. Not many people had such a close group of friends, he said, and told her that he admired her for her devotion.

"No," she told him, shaking her head. "I'm the lucky one. Mavis took me under her wing from day one." She laughed, and when he gave her an inquisitive smile, she continued. "Oh, at the very beginning, Birdie was always snapping at me, talking about how waitressing wasn't rocket science and that I needed to pick up the pace." Ben seemed very attentive and his expression encouraged her to continue. Every time his gaze met hers, her heart turned over in her chest.

"Birdie and my Nanny were very close," she said, "before Nanny passed away. She's always been a part of the family as far as I was concerned. You'd think that would mean she'd cut me a little slack. No such luck. It was quite the opposite to tell you the truth. She expected *more* of me, if anything."

He smiled and said, "You'd never know it to see you two now."

"Oh, I know! Those first few weeks she was tough on me. Mavis took up for me left and right. I can't tell you how many incorrect orders she took the blame for at the beginning. The more nervous Birdie made me, the more I messed up." As she remembered her early days working with Mavis and Birdie, her eyes filled with tears yet again. Things would never be the same, and she knew it.

"I've taken up enough of your time," she said, looking down and realizing she still had her purse and keys in her hand. He walked her out to her truck and made her promise she'd call him if anything changed. He, in turn, promised to fill

Brynn in on the details. It was likely she already knew, however, but he would make sure. As Ludie drove away towards home, she remembered that Ben had never told her what had been on his mind earlier.

# Chapter 16

The next morning Ludie arrived at the café in hopes of an update on Mavis. Just as she'd expected, Birdie had stopped by the hospital early on her way to work and had news. Melvin had maintained his vigil throughout the night, and Birdie had told him to go home and get a change of clothes and a little bit of rest. She offered to stay but he told her he'd go get some things later when Mavis was napping.

She'd had a good night, he told her. She'd slept throughout most of it, but had awakened occasionally in pain. The nurses had been prompt with her pain medications and Birdie was glad to hear it. They were in every hour through the night, turning and repositioning her, checking her breathing, giving pain medicine, swabbing her mouth to give her moisture.

Birdie sat across from Ludie and gave her a thorough report of everything Melvin had told her. Ludie looked around the café, knowing that nothing would ever be the same. She felt the tears welling up in her eyes again, and blinked them back, focusing on the busy day ahead of her. She thought of how Mavis would handle the day if she had her strength and was able to be there and began making a mental to-do list.

"Good idea," said Birdie, apparently

somehow aware of her thoughts. "We've got no business pouting around back here when we've got customers to take care of," she sniffed. "Mavis won't appreciate it one bit if word gets back to her we're neglecting her regulars." Ludie agreed, and set out to make fresh coffee and checked the tables for sugar, salt and pepper

She found that as the morning wore on staying busy helped keep her mind off her concerns. She didn't know what she'd do without her job, she thought, and suddenly her mind raced to her other job. Ben had wanted to talk to her, and it seemed important. Suppressing a painful surge of deep sadness, or perhaps disappointment, she resolved to not worry about it until she'd finished with the lunch crowd and made her way to the shop to finish out the afternoon with Ben. If he still needed her, of course. She hoped he would; she could barely imagine not being there at the shop, helping him with the candles every day. It occurred to her that it wouldn't just be the candles she would miss. She had grown truly fond of Ben and looked forward to her time working with him each day. His sense of humor was easy, and they had a good rapport. They made a good team.

It was shortly before noon when Ludie recognized a customer that came in for lunch. It was none other than Natalie Broadway, her nemesis from back in elementary school. She hadn't seen her in years, but the sight of her now made Ludie recall the feeling of all those pebbles hitting her legs as if it were yesterday.

She handed her a menu as soon as she'd taken her seat, and decided to assign Courtney that table. She didn't tell her why, just that she needed her to take that table.

"No problem," said Courtney, cheerful as always.

Courtney had a tendency to be bashful, Ludie thought, but wasn't likely to be bothered by someone she didn't even know was ever a bully. Ludie went back to looking after her customers, and was taken by surprise a few moments later when Courtney told her the lady wanted to speak to her. Natalie Broadway. Ludie frowned. *Why on earth does she want to talk to me?* She wondered.

Approaching her table with confidence, on the outside anyway, Ludie smiled. "May I help you?" she asked.

"You're Ludie, right?" Natalie asked, looking right at her.

*She knows exactly who I am,* Ludie thought. "Yep, that's me," she answered with a smile.

"I've always wondered about you," Natalie said with a tiny smile.

"Really," Ludie said, although it came out as more of a statement than a question. "Why? I've been here in town all along, never gone anywhere."

Realizing she was coming off a bit snippy, she attempted to make her tone friendlier. "Where have you been all these years?"

"I left home after high school," Natalie told

her. "I got married, but that was a mistake. I should've just stayed here in town like you did."

"Like me?" Ludie asked, her eyes wide with surprise. "Why on earth would you want that? I always dreamed of getting out of town and making something of my life."

"My life has been less than a dream," Natalie confessed. "Sometimes the best things in life are right in front of you," she continued, a wistful half-smile on her face. Now I'm back in town, staying with my aunt until I figure out what's next and where to go from here."

"Ludie…" she started, looking down at her hands. "I owe you an apology. I was never nice to you."

"Oh? I hardly even remember, besides, that was third grade, or something like that. Hardly worth mentioning," she lied. She had thought of it many times over the years, but she would never admit that.

"I was pretty bad to you in high school, too," Natalie reminded her. "I had a really bad attitude, and I treated people unfairly. You were one of those people, and I just felt like you needed to know how much I regret it."

Ludie softened at her words. Natalie had ended up being a cheerleader in high school and always had a circle of giggling, prissy friends around her, right up until the time she'd finally moved out of town. How many times she had wished they could trade places, if only for a day. Ludie had friends, as well, but they were nothing like Natalie or her friends.

186

"I was always jealous of you," Natalie went on to say.

"*Me?*" Ludie was taken aback by her confession. "Why on earth would you be jealous of me?"

"You were so smart," Natalie said, "and you were always kind to everyone. You treated people how they deserved to be treated. I treated them how the popular kids told me to treat them, and there's nothing to be proud of in that."

Ludie smiled warmly and admitted that those little rocks *had* hurt. Natalie frowned at first, saddened that she'd inflicted actual pain, and then her expression changed to laughter. "I know! You got in some pretty good shots yourself! Only *I* actually deserved it."

The two of them chatted for a few minutes, catching up on the past few years. After they'd graduated from high school, Natalie had gone off to college on a cheerleading scholarship. She'd seen it as the perfect opportunity to party and to be included in a popular sorority, but then she found herself battling alcoholism. She'd married her college sweetheart only to watch the marriage falling apart as a result of them both drinking so much. After failing her classes in the second year of college, and in light of a failed marriage, Natalie was back in Blackwater, starting her life over. Ludie was impressed by her courage, and found it easy to forgive her. She thanked her for taking the time to apologize.

"It was the right thing to do," Natalie offered. "Thank you for your forgiveness." Ludie was amazed at the healing that could take place just through resolving an old, petty conflict from years ago.

# Chapter 17

That afternoon Ludie headed for the candle shop. She was apprehensive, unsure of what Ben might say. With Mavis' admission to hospice care and the busy, eventful morning at Ladybird's, she'd managed to keep thoughts of Ben and the candle shop at bay, but now, it was all she could think of.

When she walked in, she was happy to see both Ben and Brynn working on orders. The shop smelled wonderful, and she realized with a twinge of sadness how much she loved it there. Brynn was chattering excitedly about her morning at the hospital. She was enjoying becoming a nurse more than she'd realized. When she'd first started taking classes several years ago, it was mostly because she knew she'd always need something practical to fall back on. As a single mother, the importance of security was a given. What she'd discovered on her return to school, however, was that it was not only a security net, it was her passion. She had found caring for her patients more rewarding than she'd ever thought possible.

Ben was in full support of his sister following her dreams and told her so, often.

Ludie busied herself with straightening candle displays and pretending not to listen to their conversation. Ben reassured his sister that he'd be there for her and Blake and would manage the shop as long as she needed him.

"That's what I wanted to talk to you about," Brynn said, a look of uncertainty on her face. "I love the shop. I do." She was studying Ben's face for his reaction. He waited for her response.

"I've always loved the candles and I always will," she continued. "You did so much, I wouldn't have been able to open this shop without your help," she told her brother. "I don't want you to think I'm ungrateful." She spoke of his endless hours spent building her display shelves and work tables, and how much he had helped her.

"Spit it out, Sis." He gave a little laugh, hoping to ease her discomfort. "What are you trying to say?" He pulled up a chair and sat down, gesturing at a barstool at the workspace across from him for her to sit down.

"I don't know," she breathed, pacing too much to take a seat. "I was wondering if, well…" she was hesitant to continue. "I was wondering what you'd think if I were to sell the shop and go into nursing full-time," she finished and took a deep breath. "After you left your job to come take care of the shop for me," she said, biting her lip. "All you have to do is say it's a bad idea and I won't do it."

He smiled at her, shaking his head.

"What?" she asked. "What's funny? You're mad, aren't you? Never mind," she said, pacing again, "I won't do it. I can keep the shop. There's no reason I can't stay here with you, and then just do some part-time work a couple of days a week.

I don't want you having to go back out there trying to find another job. And you sure don't want to have to work for some stranger that comes out of nowhere to buy the shop. I can work two jobs. Lots of people do that, right?"

"I'm laughing," he said, "because I can't believe you're worried about me! I'm here because I want to be." His smile was warm enough to melt butter, Ludie observed, thinking how lucky Brynn was to have a brother as supportive as Ben.

"I love it here," he said. "Who knew? I mean, it's not a job I would have ever guessed I'd be doing, but I love it. The creativity, dealing with the public, going home after a hard-day's work, satisfied with a job well done." He stood up and paced himself for a moment.

"You're right about one thing," he said. "I sure don't want to work for some stranger that doesn't know the first thing about candles."

"Oh, I know!" Brynn told him. "I get it, I do. And I won't ask you to do that. It wouldn't be fair, and I'm sorry I brought it up." A look of sadness swept over her face and she forced a smile to hide it. "The shop is my responsibility, and I will take care of it."

"I'm not going to work for a stranger, that's for sure. I have a better idea." His face lit up, an ideas clearly forming in his mind.

Brynn looked up, waiting for him to continue. "Go on."

"I want to make an offer. I want to buy the shop."

As understanding of his offer registered, her face opened up in a huge smile. "What? Do you mean it?" She clapped her hands together in delight, almost bouncing in the spot where she stood. "You could totally do it!" she was nearly shouting. "You've got Ludie!" she exclaimed. "She knows what she's doing around here, and she's great with the customers!"

Ludie's heart skipped a beat when she heard that, and she began busily straightening the candles, her hands moving quickly as she nervously avoided their expressions. *Oh, how I would love to stay here and work with Ben,* she thought. She felt a wave of discomfort at Brynn's suggestion, knowing his sister had no idea of his plans to dismiss her. This would be an awkward moment, and she knew it. It would be best to excuse herself to allow Ben a few moments to explain to his sister what his plans were. They certainly didn't need her there while they discussed all of this, she realized, and she would excuse herself.

Stepping into the workspace she congratulated Brynn on her plans and told them both she needed to go and speak with Birdie. "I haven't spoken with Birdie in a couple of hours, and I need to find out how Mavis is doing this afternoon. Besides," she continued, "I need to discuss my schedule with her. With Mavis not doing well, she may need me more than ever." Before either of them had an opportunity to stop her, she made a dash for the door, nervously dropping her keys and bending to retrieve them.

As she stepped out onto the sidewalk, she felt a sickened feeling in the pit of her stomach. She loved that shop, and it wouldn't be easy to leave. She'd chosen to tell them Birdie would need her help more often at the café in order to make it easier for Ben to tell her the truth about not needing her anymore. This would allow him to be free to make whatever plans he felt were best for the shop without having to take into consideration Ludie's employment future.

Ben watched Ludie leave the shop in a hurry and felt his excitement over buying the shop melt away. She was committed to Birdie, and he knew that. And, as if he hadn't known, she'd just made it clear to them where her devotion was. He knew he had enjoyed having her around, and her knowledge of the candles was an asset. But he had to let her do what was best for her.

His heart sank as he thought how close he'd come to telling her how he felt about her. He wanted her as a business partner, and more. Her quick, nervous departure had given him a glimpse of reality and he swallowed, trying to shake off his disappointment. He looked up to see his little sister giving him an inquisitive look.

"What's going on, Ben? What was all that about?"

"Pull up a chair," he said slowly. "We need to talk."

# Chapter 18

"This sounds serious," said Brynn. "What's going on?"

He cast his eyes downward, and his anguish was visible. Brynn worried he'd been too hasty in making the offer to buy the shop from her and was having regrets. Apparently she'd walked into a discussion he'd just been having with Ludie and even her friend knew more than she did about her own brother.

"It's about Ludie. No, it's about the shop," he corrected himself. "I want the shop, I really do. But I had hoped Ludie would want to stay and help me." He swallowed, taking in a deep breath before he began again. "But as you just witnessed, it would appear that she's devoted to Birdie and has no intentions of staying on with me." He pushed himself to his feet as if he were carrying the weight of the world on his shoulders, crossing to a worktable and began scraping wax spills off the pouring boards.

"Ben, this is not going to be an issue. You can hire someone, as scarce as jobs are these days. And you won't have any trouble training someone," she continued, laughing. "I mean, I trained you, and if *you* can be taught, anyone can." She crossed the room to turn down a spot heater that was starting to smoke. "You've got to keep the temperature down or the wax will flash. You could start a fire."

He wasn't laughing. "You're really building my confidence, Sis." He turned and looked back at her, and she recalled she hadn't seen such a dejected look on his face since their dog had run away when they were kids and didn't return.

"Oh my stars!" she said. "It's not about the shop at *all*. You don't want just an employee, or even just a partner." She allowed her subconscious thoughts to surface. "You want *Ludie*."

He looked back at her again, this time with a completely different expression on his face. He didn't even attempt to disguise his feelings. "Of course I want Ludie. I have from the beginning. But I want her to be my partner, too…" He stammered, "…in the shop, I mean." He chewed his lip nervously.

Her voice softened when she spoke again. "Ben, she's a great girl. I had my suspicions about you. Roxy and I have even talked about it. It was obvious with the way you've always smiled around her. Have you told Ludie how you feel?"

"No," he stammered, "I mean, well, I've tried." He paced across the floor, seemingly forgetting the meaningless task he was performing, looking for something to pour or scrape or trim. "I keep trying to bring it up, but something always comes up, or she changes the subject. And then, well, you saw for yourself. As soon as you started to bring up the subject again, she took off! And she mentioned yet again how she was going to be there for Birdie. I don't stand a chance."

Brynn took the scraper he was holding out of his hand and made him look at her. "You don't know where you stand until you've told her how you feel. And if you don't tell her, I will," she continued, with a grin of satisfied determination on her face.

Ben reflected on his feelings for Ludie and how much he'd enjoyed having her there. It's not that he didn't want Brynn around. After all, it was her shop and he enjoyed spending time with his sister. But Ludie… there was something different about Ludie. He reflected on the times they'd shared in recent months, in the shop, up to their elbows in wax, laughing over some creation they'd concocted or some demanding customer that had come in. He thought of the many meals they'd eaten together in the back of the shop, and how her smile warmed his heart. Ludie's laughter was the high point of his day, and he had found himself more and more often thinking of something funny and how he couldn't wait until the next day at the shop so he could share it with her.

He vowed to make sure she knew he wanted her there. Maybe she had misunderstood his intentions, just as Brynn had pointed out to him. He couldn't make any further decisions until he was sure Ludie didn't want to be here. He would have to find out, once and for all, what her plans were and what she wanted.

He spent a little more time with his sister,

and they leisurely spent the time cleaning up around the shop, making some inventory lists and merging them with custom orders to determine what was needed most.

Ludie was at the café with Birdie, thinking about the conversation between Brynn and Ben. She'd planned to go to the café to share with Birdie the feelings she'd been having about working with Ben, and now the sadness that had gripped her when she'd discovered he wasn't likely planning to keep her on. She had to put the conversation on hold, however, when she arrived to find Birdie busily chatting with customers. It was still early enough in the afternoon that there were customers lingering from after the end of the lunch rush. She occupied herself by jumping in and clearing some tables, helping some customers by refilling their glasses and tending to their needs.

While she worked, her thoughts filtered back to the conversation she'd overheard between Ben and Brynn. It was clear he had his own plans in place judging by how quickly he had responded to his sister's suggestion. He had offered to buy the shop within seconds. Ludie knew she had no right to intrude on his plans and chided herself for being so presumptuous as to insert herself into them. It would do her no good, she realized, to pour out her sob story to Birdie. For one thing, she didn't need Birdie making assumptions about her feelings for Ben and playing matchmaker; and for another thing, she didn't want Birdie to know how badly she wanted to stay at the shop and help Ben. That would only serve to make Birdie feel like working at the café with her was her second choice. She loved Birdie and never wanted to make her feel that way.

Her thoughts were interrupted when she walked past Birdie to hear her speaking to one of the regular customers about Mavis and her condition. "As much as it breaks my heart to not have Mavis here with me, it does me good to know my Ludie will be here with me."

At that moment, Ben had just walked into the Ladybird and was making his way over to Ludie to make his feelings known. Just as he neared her, he heard Birdie talking about how much she needed Ludie.

Ludie never saw Ben approaching her when she told Birdie how much she loved working at the café with her and that she wouldn't dream of working anywhere else.

Ben felt his heart sinking lower than he had thought possible and managed to step behind her as she walked past, remaining out of her line of vision. He slipped out the door, unnoticed, and walked, his movements stiff and awkward, back to the shop.

# Chapter 19

Early in the afternoon Eric Butler had flipped the pages of his day-planner, unsure of how to manipulate his schedule to accommodate the needs of his newest client. He'd already jeopardized his last contract due to his entire crew of workers abruptly leaving the site in the middle of a job. He hadn't heard from them since, which angered him deeply. He had, after all, risked a great deal by offering the work to this crew, as none of them were documented as citizens or even as contractors with temporary work visas. He'd managed to find some replacement contract employees at the last possible date in order to complete the job on deadline. Unfortunately, it had cost him a lot more money to hire legal citizens and he couldn't risk that type of thing happening again.

This newest job, he knew, was of upmost importance and if it wasn't done correctly, he wouldn't be likely to win any future bids because word would spread quickly in this one-horse town. He snapped his day planner shut and cursed beneath his breath. His thoughts went straight to Ludie, and how much she had cost him. She had too many connections in this town, and he was sure it had been her words that had nearly cost him his reputation here.

He walked down the stairs out to the sidewalk, glancing across the square to make sure her truck was parked in front of the café. Once he had seen that it was, he made his way across the street and across the courthouse lawn. He stepped into one of the gazebos, strategically taking a seat on a bench inside that would allow him a view of both the café and the candle shop but with the added benefit of a large oleander bush that would obstruct her view of him.

He watched, and waited, his coal black eyes darting back and forth. He was holding a paperback novel in front of him, but he didn't read. It was merely a prop in the event he was discovered spying on her. What he was really doing, though, was protecting his investment. His entire business and career were threatened by this unimportant small-town waitress and he wasn't altogether sure that his paternity wasn't in her hands. He'd never been fully convinced she'd actually had a miscarriage. She could very easily be lying to him, he knew. Disturbing thoughts swirled in his mind. *What if she was still carrying his child? What if she was concealing it from him?* His mind had confused the dates and he couldn't remember how long it had been, or when she had supposedly miscarried. The more he looked at his calendar, the more everything got twisted up in his mind. Would her belly even be showing evidence of the child now? The passage of time was muddled, blurred. The alcohol in his belly burned. His mind was in a fog. She was a scheming bitch, and he vowed not to succumb to her lies and manipulations. And he'd be damned if she would hide his own child from him.

Just then he caught her out of the corner of his eye, making her way toward the café from the candle shop and her look of anguish wasn't lost on him. *Why?* he wondered at that moment. *What had made her so upset?* His thoughts had been like a volcano on the verge of erupting at any moment. It was possible, he realized, that she was still carrying his child. If so, it was likely she was feeling abandoned and afraid, needing the baby's father to protect her. She missed him, and she needed him.

His emotions, an incongruent mix of disgust and sympathy, churned within him, a volatile mix that made him feel unsafe, unsteady. He struggled to remain coherent as a war raged within him, a cold sweat breaking out while he watched her, unblinking. A little while later he saw Ben leaving the shop and making his way toward Birdie's café. He was going to see her, Eric knew. A cold, hard edge cut through him, a sharp knife dividing his feelings of rage toward this unwelcome intruder that threatened to come between him and Ludie and the fierce protective instinct to protect the mother of his child.

His jaw tightened, his fist joining in as he clenched and unclenched it in rapid succession, over and over. His black eyes watched intently as the enemy opened the door of the café and entered. Eric was on his feet in an instant, springing toward the street and ready to take whatever action was necessary to protect his interests. Before he was able to cross the street, however, he saw the man leaving the cafe, a look of complete dismay on his face. Eric quickly darted behind a tree, narrowly escaping being seen.

*What just happened?* he wondered. What had she said to him? He was instantly filled with a strange satisfaction that the candle boy had been rejected, but just as quickly he choked on the bitter thought that Ludie had no right to even be interacting with another man. She was, he justified, the mother of his child. What kind of a slut was she to even be speaking to another man while she carried his child? Was there nothing sacred anymore? This would not do, he decided. Again, he was opening and closing his fist, his mind racing with thoughts of what he must do to set things straight and protect what was his.

# Chapter 20

Ludie had given up on waiting for Birdie to take a break in her conversation and busied herself with the customers. She was surprised to discover Natalie back in the café. She had spotted her in a corner booth, tucking her long, black hair behind her ear as she read a newspaper. Natalie was circling ads, Ludie realized, and went over to talk to her.

"Staying in town a while, huh?" she asked, indicating the red pen she was using to circle her ads.

Natalie looked down at the paper and smiled weakly up at Ludie. "Yeah, not much luck in the job market here, though. My aunt's been letting me stay with her while my uncle's working overseas, but I feel like I should try to get some work and make more permanent arrangements for myself."

"Why?" Ludie asked, "Is she pressuring you to move?"

"Oh. No," Natalie said, uneasily. "It's not that, I think she hardly notices me, if the truth be known. My uncle is never there, really, and she manages to entertain herself without him. My family never really understood why he married her; she's hardly ever seemed to be interested in anything other than money or power. Besides," she continued, awkwardly, "Katherine tends to, um… entertain while he's gone."

Realization dawned on Ludie so quickly she took a nervous gulp of air. "Katherine?" she asked a bit too quickly, biting her lip nervously.

"Yeah, do you know her?" Natalie asked. "She lives in a big house just outside of town, but she doesn't spend much time in Blackwater. She's the type that goes to Houston to shop and socialize."

"I know her," Ludie said. She took a seat across from Natalie and said, "We need to talk."

"How do you know her?" Natalie asked, her face full of confusion.

"Have you met Eric Butler?" Ludie asked.

"The handyman? Yeah, he seems very… *handy*," she said, wrinkling her nose. "The whole display makes me sick if you want to know the truth. My uncle is a good man, and doesn't deserve the way she treats him. He married her for love and she married him because she loved money." Natalie was clearly no fan of Katherine.

"Eric and I were living together when he started seeing her," Ludie said, biting back further comments that rested on her tongue.

A look of embarrassment and regret swept Natalie's face. "I'm so sorry, I knew she wasn't morally intact, to say the least, but I didn't know she had ruined anyone *else's* relationship."

"No," Ludie said. "It's not like that at all. Eric was not good for me. If anything, Katherine did me a favor and helped me see him for what he was before it got more dangerous."

204

"Dangerous?" Natalie looked confused. "What did he do to you?"

"That's a long story. A long and painful story. Let's just say I no longer felt safe with him, and if the truth be known I still don't feel safe. He really scared me. I just thought you should know." Her expression softened. "Whatever your feelings toward your aunt, I thought you should know the kind of person she's dealing with. He's not a nice guy."

Natalie confessed that she was ready to move out of Katherine's and find a place of her own. She was already upset over her aunt's lack of decency and her displays of bad behavior. Knowing that it wasn't just her imagination and that her Aunt Katherine had a real affair with someone who was in a relationship only made her want to get out sooner. Ludie wished her luck and told her to stay in touch. She hoped the two of them could continue talking. It really amazed her that this was the same person who had thrown rocks at her when they were children, and they were now discussing important issues as women. It was healing, in some ways.

After they'd shared such a revealing conversation, Ludie helped clean up and close the café. The last of the lunch crowd had left, and Birdie was curious about Ludie's conversation with the young lady that had come in for lunch. Ludie gave her a brief run-down and Birdie seemed glad that they'd talked. Anything that helped Ludie understand that Eric was not someone she should consider getting back with was okay by her. Ludie didn't tell Birdie about her pregnancy or the abuse, of course. Poppa and the good old boys' club in town would break laws that only the good old boys' club could cover up. Ludie laughed at the pictures her mind conjured.

After they'd closed up, Ludie needed to talk, and had to be careful what she shared with Birdie. She wasn't comfortable talking about it to Brynn at the moment, because she didn't want to create anything awkward between her and Ben. Regardless of her feelings about her future with the shop, she didn't want to come between a brother and sister. There was no job that was worth that.

She got into her truck and turned down Roxy's street. She was just the perfect person to talk to, Ludie knew. When she rang the doorbell, Roxy answered the door almost immediately. In typical Roxy style, she was dressed in cashmere and diamonds. Always first class, never less. She always had her makeup applied perfectly. She was a woman used to being pampered, and never considered it an over-indulgence to take good care of herself. Ludie could stand to learn from her. When she'd come over from Australia, she'd definitely brought a touch of class and a flair for fashion. Her move had apparently had something to do with the lingerie business but Ludie was never sure exactly what she did. She shrugged it off and focused on the situation at hand.

"Come on in, Luv. I was just thinking about you." She held the door open wide and motioned her in. She offered Ludie a glass of white wine which she accepted, knowing it was one of those kinds of nights that a few sips of a nice wine would be great. Ludie kicked her shoes off and sat on the sofa, curling her feet up beneath her. Best to be comfortable, she thought. Roxy returned to the living room with two tall goblets of chilled wine and sat down near her.

"That bad, is it?" she asked. "Talk to me, Luv, you'll feel better. Let Dr. Roxy help you," she said, and they both giggled.

Ludie told her everything. Once she got started, it was as though a dam had been released and she poured out her whole story, her tears flowing freely. She told her about Ben and the changes at the shop, with him planning to buy it from his sister. She told her about Mavis and how she was barely clinging to life. She spoke until her throat was raw. The wine was crisp, but not dry. It was just the right wine for the occasion, which didn't surprise Ludie at all. In addition to that, she'd served a beautiful tray of fruits and fancy cheeses and crackers. It was so like Roxy to have the best of everything, always. She had been successful in life, but managed to remain down to earth, never considering anyone to be beneath her. Until, of course, they hurt someone she loved.

"Well," purred Roxy, leaning over to pat her friend on the knee, "it's clear to me that you're in love. And if you don't wake up and see this bloke is mad about you as well, you're a fool. A blind fool. As for Mavis, you've got to go down there and just look her in the eye and tell her how you feel about her. Don't leave things unsaid. And for Eric, like I said, you let Aunt Roxy take care of everything." Her lips curved in a smile of extreme satisfaction.

"I thought it was 'Dr. Roxy'," Ludie laughed.

"That's what I said." She turned up her glass and finished the last of her wine. "Just let me handle it." With that, she reached under her coffee table and withdrew her laptop. Opening it on the coffee table, she pulled up a site for online floral orders. She made quick work of placing an order, pausing to open another browser to secure the address she needed.

Katherine would be receiving a beautiful arrangement the next day, and the card would read, "*My dearest Amy, thank you for a wonderful evening and for pleasures I hadn't known. All my love, Eric.*"

"Who is Amy?" Ludie asked, her eyes widened in surprise.

"Hell if I know," she shrugged. "But I'd love to watch Katherine while she tries to figure that out, and Eric while he tries to explain flowers he didn't send intended for a woman he doesn't even know."

Ludie shook her head, not even to pretend she wasn't amused. "You know I'd be trying to talk you out of all this insanity if it didn't make me feel so much better."

"Well that's the whole point, really, isn't it, Luv?" she answered. "Now, you've had your wine and some nice fruit and cheese and you've gotten all your drama out. I believe you've got something to do now," she continued. "Go and see Mavis, and tell her how you feel about her." Ludie hugged her when she left. How did Roxy always know the right things to say and do?

Eric sat across the street and down a couple of houses, his car turned off, watching and waiting. She was with that damned redhead, and he knew the two of them were talking about him. He wondered what they were saying. He wouldn't be surprised at all if the woman was encouraging Ludie to keep the baby from him. His eyes burned as he watched the door, never taking his eyes off it except to observe a woman pushing a stroller down the sidewalk past his car. The stroller was empty as there was a toddler walking along right in front of the woman. A few short feet in front of them was another small child of about three years of age, he was guessing. He was riding a bike with training wheels, and his mother was laughing with joy while watching her children. *I know what she's laughing about,* he thought. *She's enjoying her children while excluding their father from their lives.* I know how the poor guy feels. There was no respect for men amongst women of this caliber, and he was seeing it far more often as of late.

He refocused his cold, dark stare on Roxy's front door and it wasn't long before Ludie emerged. He waited until she was in her truck and had started it before he turned the keys in his own ignition. Giving her just enough time to back out of the driveway and pull away, he pulled out from the curbside and began to follow at a distance. He didn't know where she was going, but he had no doubt it somehow involved him and her plot to exclude him. The secrets she kept would be exposed, he vowed, and she would pay for her mistakes.

It wasn't long before he saw her pulling into the hospital parking lot and parking her truck. When she got out, she walked slowly toward the entrance with her head down. She seemed emotional, it occurred to him, and his thoughts began to swirl, trying to get inside her head and examine her evil plots against him. She would not get away with this. Whatever she was doing at the hospital, he didn't like it. Was she planning for the birth? Was she meeting with adoptive parents and introducing them to her doctor? He wondered. Was she planning on getting rid of the baby? There was certainly no lack of doctors who were willing to do any procedure requested in order to make money. If she was considering that, he would kill her. She would not get rid of his baby, he decided, and she would not just give it away to someone wanting to adopt. She would not give away something that belonged to him. He would ensure that didn't happen.

Ludie made her way toward the hospital entrance, steeling herself and trying to draw from her inner strength to face Mavis and say her goodbyes. According to Poppa and Birdie, she wasn't doing well at all. It had been nearly two days since she'd opened her eyes long enough to make eye contact and speak. She seemed weaker and weaker by the day, they'd said.

As Ludie entered the building, she breathed a sigh of relief. She was here, and she would face it. She'd had a vague feeling of uncertainty the whole way over from Roxy's house. It was a sense of dread that permeated to her core. It felt almost as if a strong impending sense of doom was oppressing her, but the feeling lifted once she'd entered the hospital. She supposed it was better because she was here now, and she'd come too far to go back. She would sit at Mavis's bedside and tell her how much she meant to her.

When Ludie stepped into Mavis's room, she took one look at her and knew it was bad. Birdie had been right, she realized. It wouldn't be long at all. She sensed it.

"Mavis," she whispered, leaning over to kiss her. Mavis's eyelids fluttered the slightest bit, and a small, weak moan escaped her lips. "It's me. Ludie. I just wanted you to know… I love you. You've been more than a friend to me. You were there for me when I lost my Nanny." She gave a small uncomfortable laugh. "You protected me from Birdie."

She held Mavis's hand in hers and noticed how terribly frail and weak it was. Taut skin stretched to cover her swollen hands and fingers, just as the skin on her face was drawn tightly over her facial bones. She hadn't realized it would be like that. She was surprised to see that Mavis slept with her mouth open, and her eyelids were slightly open, revealing her eyes underneath heavy lids. Her eyes didn't seem to focus on anyone or anything. They blankly stared ahead, making Ludie wonder if she was really even there with her at all. As if in answer to her question, Mavis squeezed her hand so gently she almost thought she imagined it.

A nurse came in twice while she was there and placed a syringe dropper with red liquid on her bottom lip and squeezed it beneath her tongue. It was to keep the pain under control, she explained.

Ludie sat next to her bed for the longest time, holding her hand, gently stroking her brow. She talked to her, talked to her of some of their greatest times together. She leaned over and kissed her at times, pausing from her stories long enough to fuss over her, rearranging her pillow and her hands in an effort to make her more comfortable. She spoke through her tears, but drew a great deal of comfort knowing she'd said everything she wanted to say to her dear friend. When she finally got up to leave, it had long since been dark. The hour was late, but she was pleased that her feeling of impending doom was no longer hanging over her when she left. She was certain it must have lifted when she'd spoken to Mavis and revealed her feelings. It had felt good to tell her. She hadn't left things unsaid.

Outside, Eric watched her leave, wishing he'd gone in to observe her. *Who was she with and what was she doing?* It was too late in the evening for a doctor's appointment, he reasoned. She'd been up to something, he was sure. He would get to the bottom of it, and it wouldn't take him long. He watched her when she started her truck and pulled away, then followed at a safe distance long enough to see that she was turning toward the road that led to the farmhouse. He was relieved and decided not to follow after her. She would be safe tonight and besides, he needed to go home and rest. He had a lot of preparations to make. He breathed a long sigh of contentment. It would all work out and he would be the one to make it happen.

# Chapter 21

When Ludie got to the farmhouse she found Poppa waiting up. She put some water on the stove for tea and went into the living room and told him she wanted to talk to him. He followed her back to the kitchen and took a seat across from her.

"I saw Mavis. She looks bad, Poppa."

"I know. I went and saw her this morning with Birdie. Melvin didn't look so great either. He wasn't there when you went by?"

"No," she smiled. "It was just me and Mavis. I talked to her for a long time. She knew I was there, I think. Do you think that's silly?" She eyed him expectantly while she waited for him to answer.

"No, Mouse. I don't. I'm sure she *did* know you were there. You mean a lot to her. Always have. What did you say to her?"

The tea kettle whistled to let her know the water was ready and she got up and rummaged in the cabinet looking for tea bags while she talked.

"I told her I loved her, of course. I told her how much she meant to me, and how knowing she and Nanny were friends made me feel closer to her." She looked up at Poppa and concern flashed across her face. "I didn't mean she took

Nanny's *place,* I promise!" She was bobbing the tea bag up and down furiously in her cup, matching the pace of her racing thoughts.

"No," he chuckled, "I didn't think you did. And your Nanny would have been glad Mavis was there for you. They talked about it when Nanny faced her own cancer."

Her mouth opened in surprise and she looked up from the business of making hot tea. "Really?" She smiled when he nodded that yes, they had. There was something truly special about being loved like that, and she was thankful her Nanny had loved her so much she'd wanted to have someone else looking after her. When she accepted Mavis and Birdie into her life as grandmother figures, she knew she had much reason to be grateful. God had blessed her richly, and she knew it.

"Poppa," she said slowly, turning around to face him, bringing her cup to her mouth and blowing on the tea. "Since we're talking, I was wondering…" He looked up at her and waited for her to continue. The steam rose and curled from her cup and she blew softly, dispersing it into a whisper.

"You and Birdie…" she trailed off, hoping she was not being intrusive.

His silver moustache moved, doing little to disguise his smile. "What about me and Birdie?"

"Poppa, stop that! I know that you know what I'm talking about. I just think you don't want me to know," she said, frustrated.

"Oh you *know* all that, do you?" His laugh

frustrated her further. "I have enjoyed her company a great deal, Ludie. I don't know what you want me to say."

"I want you to tell me if there's more to it than that. I love Birdie, and she deserves to have someone special in her life, just as you do. All I'm saying is, you two have been spending an awful lot of time together lately, and, well, I just think that…" she trailed off, not knowing exactly *what* she thought.

Poppa helped her out. "Like I said, Mouse, I have enjoyed her company. Sometimes it just feels good for me to have someone to talk to now that you're all grown up and staying busy. But no one will ever take your Nanny's place. Just like you said you weren't trying to replace her, neither am I."

"Oh, Poppa I know that!" She rushed over to him, pulling a chair out and sitting directly in front of him. "I know that. But it doesn't mean you shouldn't have someone to keep you company." She smiled warmly. "And I think Nanny would have more than approved of your choice. She pretty much hand-picked Birdie and Mavis to be part of our lives, didn't she?" They both laughed, knowing that it wouldn't be out of character for her to have made choices that would be in their best interest long after she was gone.

Poppa's expression quickly grew serious. "Ludie, you know she was the love of my life. She was my sweetheart and that will never change." He leaned back in his chair, smiling at the memories, and went on. "I'll never forget when we

216

brought your Daddy home, wrapped in that little blue blanket. He was the best thing she ever could have given me." Ludie's heart ached as she tried to grasp how it would feel to look into the eyes of her own infant child. She enjoyed hearing about how much joy it had brought Nanny and Poppa, however, and wondered how things would be if her own parents had survived. Or her baby, she thought sadly.

"I didn't think anything would ever bring us more joy until your Daddy came home from his job in town one day with a pretty young girl by his side," he said. "She was the prettiest thing, your Mama. She came in here with that pretty brown ponytail bouncing along. We'd never seen him happier."

Then his eyes misted over. "And he never was, until they came home with a sweet little girl of their own wrapped up in a pink blanket. Your Nanny was on cloud nine. It's a wonder any of us ever got to hold you; she wouldn't put you down."

Ludie hung on every word of the conversation. It made her feel complete, hearing about what it had been like when they were a family. Her heart felt raw, and yet whole for the first time. She knew she'd been part of an amazing family, and knew also that family wasn't always determined by genetics or marriage. God had again blessed her with a wonderful family. Poppa, and Birdie, and Mavis were her family. Even Melvin had become her family by default, because he loved Mavis so much.

Her heart tightened in her chest when she

thought of Brynn and Ben and Blake, and how they had made her feel like she was a part of their family also. She looked down, her eyelashes casting shadows on her cheeks. Poppa reached down and wiped a tear away. "Now you stop the crying. You've still got a family that loves you. You have always been loved, my little mouse, and you always will be. The good Lord doesn't ever take away something and not give you something else you need." This time Poppa was the one with the tears escaping, and she held him for a long time in the warm kitchen that held so many memories.

The next morning the shrill ringing of the phone pierced the silence in the old farmhouse, waking both Ludie and Poppa. It was Birdie, and she was at the hospital. The time was drawing closer, and the hospice nurse had told her it was time to call the family in.

In less than half an hour Poppa and Ludie were rushing down the hall toward Mavis's room. Birdie and Melvin were at her bedside. Mavis had a mask on her face with green elastic bands on each side, pressing into her cheeks. Birdie rearranged them, adjusting the mask to make her more comfortable. She wouldn't be happy unless she was fidgeting over her friend and no one tried to stop her. There was a clear bag attached to the bottom of the mask and it seemed to stay full while the oxygen was being pumped in through the tubing. Mavis's eyes were open, but her stare was fixed somewhere near the point where the wall met the ceiling. Her pupils didn't move. Ludie reached down to touch her hand and noticed that

218

her skin was hot.

Just then a nurse walked in with two syringes, each with a small amount of liquid. It was Morphine and Ativan, she told them. One would help the pain and the other would slow down her rapid breathing and heart rate.

Ludie felt lost, not knowing what to expect and needing some guidance. She broke down and called Brynn, who seemed relieved to hear from her until she detected the fear in her voice.

"I'll be right there," she said, once Ludie had told her what was happening. "I'm so glad you called."

Ludie wasn't surprised when she came rushing in within thirty minutes of her phone call. She rushed to her side and gave her a hug, then went straight to Mavis, assessing her condition. She turned back to Ludie and nodded. It was a gesture that spoke volumes.

"Not long," she whispered, so softly that Ludie had to read her lips. The two embraced, then Brynn went on to explain how the medications were helping and why it was better for patients who were at this stage not to receive IV fluids. Fluid and nutrition, apparently, tended to do little more than feed the cancer. Dehydration had actually been proved to increase rather than decrease comfort levels, she explained.

Brynn pulled back the covers gently and checked Mavis's hands and feet. They appeared purple, mottled, and felt very cold to the touch, after being so hot moments before. Apparently that assessment meant something in particular to

Brynn judging by her expression. It felt good to have Brynn there, and Ludie told her so.

It was early in the morning when Mavis took her last breath. The sun had barely come up over the horizon in Blackwater, Texas when Mavis Ann Simmons left this world to go to her reward. Melvin was lost, and accepted the comfort offered by the loving family that surrounded him.

Three days later they embraced again at the cemetery, and each of them took their turn to place a single yellow rose on top of her coffin. Yellow roses had been her favorite, and Melvin called her his yellow rose when he was overtaken by sobs.

Ludie felt the loss deeply and focused on work to help her get through. Birdie was business as usual at the café, as far as everyone could tell. Ludie caught her wiping her eyes with a handkerchief she kept in her pocket on several occasions but true to Birdie's nature, she didn't want any attention on her. There was work to do, she protested, and they had little choice but to honor her wishes.

Ludie spoke to Birdie on Natalie's behalf and she was now being trained by Tyler and Courtney, which amused everyone to no end. When Ludie brought it up, Birdie had clicked her tongue at her, reminding her that Mavis had trained them, which made them more than competent. Natalie was no longer staying with her aunt. Apparently she'd made other arrangements and not long after, she'd discovered that

Katherine was staying in her condo in the city more. She'd invested all that time and money into renovating the house and had then grown bored of it, as she tended to do. She'd play with something like a cat would, giving it her full interest until it stopped moving, only to end up batting it away like an unwanted toy.

Ludie began speaking with Brynn more often, and eventually conversation turned to the reasons she was no longer helping out at the shop. They were having lunch with Roxy one day in a corner booth at Ladybird's. Ludie couldn't tell Brynn how much she missed Ben and wished she was still working with him. She couldn't admit how much she always enjoyed it and how much fun he was to be around, so she just kept quiet, until Brynn brought it up one day.

"Ben was pretty disappointed when you left," she told her. "He keeps asking me what he did wrong that made you want to leave." The heavy lashes that shadowed Ludie's cheeks flew up.

"What?"

Brynn told her he'd been a wreck ever since the day she quit and wondered what he might have done to make her want to leave.

"But," Ludie stammered. "He said he wanted to talk to me, and it sounded pretty serious. I understood, of course, if he couldn't keep me on at the shop, but it still hurt," she confessed.

"What do you mean he couldn't keep you on at the shop? He's done nothing but mope around the place because you're not there."

"But he said he wanted to talk to me, what was that about?"

"Ludie, he *did* need to talk to you, and I would say it was definitely serious. He wanted to make you his partner. And I don't think he meant just at the shop, either."

"Oh no," Ludie breathed, bringing her hands to her cheeks. *Why did they suddenly feel so hot?* she wondered. "Brynn," she said. "Oh, Brynn! We need to talk!"

When Ludie finally opened up and revealed her feelings for Ben and how terribly she'd missed the candle shop, Brynn was thrilled. She hated seeing her brother upset day after day. She was going to be graduating very soon and was feeling guiltier by the day that he seemed so lost. His original enthusiasm about buying the shop had diminished, and Brynn had felt helpless to do anything about it.

Roxy was conspicuously quiet throughout the whole conversation, her eyes darting back and forth between her two friends, soaking up every word. She was no less thrilled than Brynn and, finally, they both gave Ludie an ultimatum. "You tell him or we will." At that, Ludie laughed nervously, wondering how she was going to bring herself to tell him.

As it turned out, Brynn had apparently paved the way quite smoothly. When Ludie walked into the shop the next day, Ben looked up, a broad smile stretching across his face.

"You're back!" he smiled, "and not a

moment too soon." He spoke quickly, emphatically, never stopping the task at hand. He began pouring candles into the dozens of glass jars that were across every available inch across the surface of the largest work table. "I should dock your pay, 'Little Miss No-Call, No-Show,'" he laughed. He began to outline for her the orders that were keeping him so busy, with no one to help. As he spoke, he continued rapidly scooping a metal pouring pitcher into the melting pot, and pouring the molten wax into the jars, rotating them as he went. "I mean, Blake helps me, but he's a kid. And he has school. The kid can only do so much, you know. Child labor laws."

Ludie smiled, watching him as he worked, and listening equally hard while he tried to make her understand why he needed her so badly. He was rambling and scarcely took a breath. She was barely able to suppress her laughter as she watched him nervously continue.

"Yes," she told him.

"Yes, what?" He finally stopped, turning to meet her gaze anxiously.

"Yes, I'll come back. Yes, I'll help you. But only because you need me so badly." She craned her neck forward to take in all the candles he'd worked so feverishly to pour.

"That's what I've been trying to tell you," he said, smiling his relief. "I've been trying to tell you why I need you back."

"I know why you need me back," she laughed, "and it's not a moment too soon. I've just stood here and watched you pour dozens of candles. Clear candles. With no scent." He snapped his head around to look at the fruits of his labor only to realize he'd been pouring and scooping clear, unscented wax straight from the melting pot without blending in any dye or mixing in any fragrance oils.

"I'd say you need me back pretty badly," she said. "The customers won't like their candles like this. It's a wonder you didn't go out of business without me here."

"I was doing just fine until you walked in here and distracted me," he said. "You're the reason I made a mis-pour," he laughed, and crossed the room and hugged her tightly, not in the least bit aware or concerned that he would smear wax on her clothes. "I should fire you for distracting me."

She smiled with her cheek pressed against his chest, and cherished the feeling of being in his arms.

# Chapter 22

Ludie and Ben grew closer over the following weeks and found a new and heightened joy in working together. They were both amazed at how compatible they were now that they didn't have to deal with Eric being constantly in her life. He had seemed to slack off and hadn't made his presence known lately.

Ben and Ludie had dinner at Roxy's from time to time. She'd invited them occasionally, in order to have another couple there, "to keep it from being awkward" with just her and Dennis having dinner at her place. The two of them had grown close as well, and everyone was as supportive of them as they were of Ludie and Ben, but Roxy had a fear of commitment. She wasn't ready, she argued, and was afraid if she spent too much time alone with him he'd lose his mind and press her for more than she was ready to give. Ludie found a great deal of amusement in that fear, knowing that Roxy had Dennis wrapped around her little finger and that he would do anything she wanted.

It was at one of these dinners that the subject of Eric came up. Ludie had needed something from the car and was nearly to the door when Ben offered to get it for her. She suppressed a shiver, but Ben had noticed. "You're still afraid of him, aren't you?" he asked, already knowing the answer.

"He doesn't bother me anymore," she told him, "but sometimes I just get the feeling someone's watching me."

"I wouldn't worry too much about that," Roxy shouted from the kitchen. "My guess is he's terrified to even come near you."

Dennis and Ben both snapped their heads and shot darts into her with their eyes. Ludie couldn't help but notice.

"What?" asked Roxy, innocently. "I didn't say anything."

"Well you have now," Ben snapped.

"She has what?" Ludie asked, looking at each of them in turn. "What does everyone here know that I don't?" she demanded.

"You shouldn't hear from Eric," Ben answered with a deep sigh, "because Dennis and I had a little talk with him."

"You *what*?" she demanded. "Why?"

"He was watching you," Ben answered, "and Roxy saw him. Neither of us was going to let him get away with that." They shared the details with her, and she felt her blood grow cold at the knowledge that he'd continued to watch her long after she'd thought the issue was resolved and that he'd moved on.

Roxy promised she hadn't created any more vengeful acts and that she'd stopped only because the guys had told her to, out of concern that any reminders could provoke someone as psychotic as Eric to action.

In the following weeks Ludie managed to stay fairly busy and was able to keep her mind off him for the most part. She'd spent a great deal of time with Poppa and Birdie, sharing their grief over Mavis but at the same time enjoying the openness of their budding relationship.

Brynn's graduation ceremony was nearing, and Ludie and Roxy planned a graduation party for her at the café. Ben and Dennis helped, knowing it would mean a lot to her that they were all so proud of her. Blake was involved as well, and he'd promised to keep quiet and not let the surprise slip to his Mom.

When the day of the ceremony arrived, they all gathered at the auditorium early and took places near the front row. When it was Brynn's turn to cross the stage, they all jumped to their feet shouting and applauding, even louder than the families of the other new nurses. When the instructor pinned her, her hands were shaking, and Ludie thought she was probably jumpy because she wasn't sure when the enthusiastic group near the front row would have another outburst.

After the ceremony, they suggested stopping by Birdie's for pie and coffee. Ludie told them she had a key and that it wouldn't be a problem. When they approached the door of the quiet, dark café, Ludie turned the key in the lock and flipped the lights on. At that moment dozens of their nearest and dearest friends jumped out and yelled "Hellooooo, nurse!" Brynn nearly doubled over in laughter, amazed that her friends would go to such lengths.

She fussed at them for having a surprise party, reminding them that surprise parties were for birthdays, not graduations. They reminded her she wasn't Emily Post anymore, she was Florence Nightingale now, and she laughed even more, thrilled at the incredible show of support of her friends.

The party for Brynn somehow brought Ben and Ludie even closer together. He was touched at all the effort she'd put into making sure his sister knew how much they all supported her. They were doing very well together at work, and their relationship lent an atmosphere of romance to the shop, which could only mean success in the business of candles.

In addition to their success in the business, their relationship seemed to thrive under the approval of their families. Brynn and Blake both loved Ludie, and Poppa and Birdie made no secret of the fact that they approved of Ben and knew he was good for her.

By the beginning of summer, Ben had brought up the subject of marriage. Ludie was shocked, at first, and then quickly grew used to the idea. This was all unfolding so much more comfortably than her relationship with Eric ever had, and it was nice not having to be so cautious in everything she said and did.

The first time she'd stayed overnight with Ben, she'd almost panicked when he entered to find her relaxing on his unmade bed. Instead of being upset, though, he'd jumped right in the middle of the bed and started tickling her. They'd finally collapsed, breathless with laughter, when he suddenly leaned down and kissed her. Her heart leapt with joy when she realized he hadn't kissed her on the lips, but just above them on her scar. Tenderly. The expression of love in his eyes told her he loved her, truly loved her, exactly the way she was.

In spite of how quickly the two of them comfortably settled into their relationship, and how her heart fluttered every time she saw him, she was still surprised when one day she felt a familiar wave of unique nausea overtake her while mixing fragrance oils one day at work. She had felt that way once before, and she knew instantly what it meant. This time, however, she didn't sneak quietly away on her own and purchase a pregnancy test, terrified of being discovered. This time, she bravely announced her suspicions to Ben and he'd picked her up, spinning her around in his arms.

They went together to buy the home pregnancy test, and he stood next to her in the bathroom as they counted down the minutes to watch the strip turn colors. When it did, they both shouted their joy. It was right this time, and she knew it. She wished she would've been married *before* having a child, and knew Nanny had taught her better. In her heart, however, she knew Ben was the one for her and she couldn't wait to be his wife and the mother of his child.

They approached Birdie and Poppa with great reluctance, fearing their reactions. They were at first met with a lecture on how things were supposed to be done. When Poppa informed Ben that well-behaved young ladies didn't find themselves expecting babies without benefit of marriage, he was quickly told that Ben wouldn't need a shotgun to "encourage" him down the aisle. Ben looked Poppa directly in the eyes when he told him how he wanted nothing more than to marry this beautiful young lady and that he'd loved her since the day he'd found her in the shop with his sister. He managed to catch Ludie's Poppa alone for a few moments and officially asked for her hand in marriage.

"I was already planning to ask you," he stammered, "and then, well, you know."

Poppa responded that he would be delighted to give him her hand in marriage, and Ben quietly began discussing his ideas for a proposal.

Once they were all back in the same room, Poppa and Birdie made it clear that Ludie had been brought up with traditional values and made it clear that a wedding would need to take place in the near future. Birdie began excitedly chattering about wedding plans and Poppa kept trying to hush her. He even agreed when Birdie informed him with a whisper that he'd need to wear a tuxedo and not his fancy coveralls to walk his beautiful granddaughter down the aisle. Reluctantly at first, he ended up agreeing to follow all of Birdie's requests, or demands, in order to make his granddaughter proud of him on her wedding day.

Ben realized a proposal wouldn't even be necessary. The wedding, he was thrilled to know, was going to happen.

# Chapter 23

Spring had long since given way to summer and wedding plans were well in full force by the time summer was ready to yield to fall. Ludie's belly was growing rapidly, and she and Ben delighted in the changes taking place. He had fallen asleep twice while lying on the couch with his head near Ludie's lap, his hand across her belly waiting for a kick. He was delighted each time he felt it, and had already begun thinking of names. Benjamin seemed to be one of his first choices and he often referred to the baby as "Little Ben" until the day an ultrasound revealed the baby was a girl.

One afternoon not long after the ultrasound they were at the shop, Ludie watching him from a chair with her feet elevated on boxes while he poured candles. She held a baby book of names in her lap, calling out names to him as she found some that she liked. He teased her, coming up with outrageous names no one had named their babies since the Middle Ages.

"What was your Nanny's name?" he asked, taking a break from his task to look over at her.

"Anne," she told him, remembering her fondly. "That was Mavis's middle name, too, except she didn't have an 'e' at the end."

"That's it!" he exclaimed, rushing over to

Ludie and bending down to speak to her growing tummy. "Hello, Annie. This is your Daddy and I just wanted you to know I love you and your Mommy so much!" While he was on his knees in front of her, speaking to their baby and caressing her stomach, he reached into his pocket and retrieved the most beautiful ring she'd ever seen. "I want your Mommy to do me the honor of becoming my wife. Ludie Blackwell, will you marry me?"

Ludie's eyes filled with tears, happier than she'd ever thought was possible. *Annie.* She was having a baby girl, and her name would be Annie. And she was going to marry Annie's Daddy! They spent the rest of the day referring to the baby by name, and found themselves more excited than ever at the idea of their upcoming wedding and beginning of their family.

Brynn was thriving in her new career, and equally excited about the wedding plans and the idea of becoming an aunt. Roxy demanded equal billing and wasn't the least bit shy about inserting herself into the plans at every opportunity. Ludie was thrilled at having Brynn as a sister-in-law and realized Roxy was nearly every bit as close to being an aunt as Brynn. She thrived on the excitement generated by both of them.

As she neared her due date, she also neared her wedding date. There was even some debate as to which would occur first. Birdie issued threats that she'd better not have that baby before they were legal, and Ben and Ludie laughed them off but still continued their plans as quickly as they could.

One day they headed to the café for lunch, turning the sign around in the window of the shop that read "*Closed for lunch, back at 1:00 pm.*" When they walked in the door at the Ladybird, they were fully expecting another lecture from Birdie and a rolling of the eyes from Poppa, who was now a regular fixture in the diner.

Instead they were met with a cloud of balloons and all their friends, including customers from both the Ladybird Cafe and Blackwater Creek Candle Company. Small Texas towns had long ago defined the natural order of things. It was marriage first, and then babies, and Ludie would be no exception. Birdie had laid out the law and no one even tried to argue with her anymore. So it shouldn't have come as a surprise to walk in on an old-fashioned "bridal shower-slash-baby shower." She thought all the little old hens of Blackwater would surely be cackling and gossiping by now, but on the contrary they were all there, more than happy to be taking part in an upcoming wedding *and* the birth of a new baby.

From his familiar perch in a gazebo across the courthouse lawn, Eric Butler watched the festivities. He had kept his distance for as long as he could after those two goons had confronted him. They had made their point, and he'd stayed away, for a while. It was only a matter of time, however, before he'd been unable to focus his thoughts on anything except the mother of his child. He couldn't bear another man being anywhere near her, and he would not cave to threats. It was *his* child she carried, and he'd returned to his apartment in Blackwater after an extended absence with every intention of claiming what was his.

When he ventured out to his familiar perch in the gazebo, he saw that it was not the normal lunch rush in the café. *His* café, he reminded himself. He had been the one who had renovated that café, and they were inside, celebrating. Without him. The corner of his mouth twisted in anger. They'd told him she had lost his child, and for a time, he had believed them. It had seemed the longest time, but then he'd known they were lying. They just didn't want him to be a part of his child's life, and he was not going to give in so easily to their demands. She was the mother of his child, after all. He was going to be a part of her life, whether they liked it or not. He pulled a long drink from a silver flask he kept inside his jacket, then grimaced when he felt the acid burn in his esophagus.

He moved quietly, and with stealth. He darted from behind one tree to take his place behind another closer one. As he drew closer, careful not to be observed, he discovered the source of the celebration. He looked between a sea of pink balloons that had parted slightly to see Ludie posing for a photo behind a table with a huge cake with pink and white frosting, with the candle boy's hand across her swollen belly.

His face twisted with rage at the sight of this man with his hands on Ludie and his growing child. Even as he watched, murderous plans began to hatch in his mind. As quickly as he'd arrived, he left, remaining careful not to be seen, and headed back to his apartment to finalize his plans.

Inside, Ludie and Ben beamed at the beautiful gifts they were opening. They were touched at the love and support they were being given and Ben held up an empty iced tea glass and clinked it with a butter knife, calling their guests to attention. Together they gave a sweet thank you speech, and then said they had an announcement.

"In honor of Ludie's beloved Nanny, Anne Blackwell, and her dear friend, Mavis Ann Simmons, we'd like to announce the impending arrival of our sweet daughter, Anne, who we'll be calling 'Annie.'" The crowd shouted their approval, and Ludie glanced over to see Poppa and Birdie exchanging a look, both with tear-filled eyes.

Roxy promptly announced that the last four letters in her name were a-n-n-e. Not to be outdone, Brynn cleared her throat loudly, and looked meaningfully across the room at her brother, who laughed out loud in response. Ludie and some of the others looked to them for an explanation, and Blake provided the needed answer. "My Mom's middle name is Ann! She's really 'Brindalynn Ann!'"

At this, everyone laughed and clinked their punch cups in a toast to sweet little Annie, who would be the darling of the town.

Later on, after all the festivities, Ben and Ludie walked back to the shop, holding hands, both still giddy with excitement. Her due date was approaching within a month and the wedding was sooner, set for the coming weekend. She had just been informed that she'd be going to Houston the next day with Brynn and Roxy, partly on the instructions of Birdie, to find a wedding gown.

When the next morning arrived, Ludie was waiting when Roxy came to pick them up. She went with them, even though she didn't feel a traditional gown was necessary. Especially a *maternity* wedding gown. Did they even make those? Roxy and Brynn had disagreed and were taking her to a specialty salon in Houston. When they arrived, Ludie was pleasantly surprised. It was a bridal and lingerie boutique with the loveliest of designs. Ludie didn't think it was possible but at the insistence of her friends and bridesmaids, they conducted an intense search and were rewarded with a beautiful maternity wedding gown.

While they were there, they'd stepped over and were eyeing some very sexy lingerie. Ludie was surprised to see they even made maternity lingerie and allowed Roxy to help her select some items.

"Nothing will fit me," she protested. "Or haven't you noticed I look like a watermelon with arms and legs?"

"Oh hush," ordered Roxy. "There is no one more beautiful than a woman glowing with pregnancy. It's sexy, and besides, you have every reason to wear something lovely and feminine. Men find their women at their sexiest when they're in seductive lace, ripe with child."

Ludie and Brynn exchanged a look and both burst into laughter.

"Ripe?" asked Ludie.

"Trust me," Roxy snapped. "I know my lingerie." At this, Ludie recalled that Roxy's line of business had something to do with lingerie designs and sales. She'd never been quite sure exactly what Roxy did for a living, only that she'd always seemed to have the most beautiful lingerie draped on every piece of furniture in her home and that she spent a lot of time on the internet and excusing herself to deal with business calls. She sewed an awful lot, too. Dennis must consider himself a lucky man, Ludie imagined.

"All right, lingerie woman, if you think you can make me look sexy in my current condition, go for it."

"That's more like it, Luv," she said, making her way to rack after rack of divine creations of lace. "Aha! Here we are," she said, removing a beautiful black lace design and holding it up to Ludie for size. "Go on," she urged. "Try it on."

Ludie had to admit it was breathtaking, and made her way to the fitting room to try it on, hoping she could make it fit over her giant expanding belly. Stepping into the fitting room, she removed it from its delicate hanger and noticed the designer tag inside. Glancing at it to see what size it was she noted the words.

"*Roxy of Brisbane*" the label read, and she screamed as the realization of what it meant dawned on her. Roxy was a designer! On the other side of the door, her shout was met with peals of laughter. "Ah, you've figured me out, have you, Luv?"

# Chapter 24

That evening she returned home, careful not to let Ben see any of her new lingerie and certainly not her wedding gown. In keeping with tradition, he would see none of it until the wedding night.

Ludie and Ben drove to the farmhouse together to sit down with Poppa and Birdie and have some dinner, then finalize some of the plans for the wedding. Birdie was amazingly organized, and Ludie could barely suppress tears of joy at the amount of time and money that had been put into her wedding. Poppa had been extremely supportive, and generous.

Shortly after 10:00 o'clock, Birdie glanced up to see Ludie stifling a yawn, her eyelids heavy with fatigue. "Take your bride home, Ben. She needs her rest."

Helping Ludie to her feet, Ben gave her a kiss and wrapped an arm around her, letting her lean her head on his shoulder. He shook Poppa's hand and thanked Birdie for all her hard work. Ludie gave them both hugs and walked with Ben out to the car.

As they drove past the candle shop on their way home, Ludie happened to glance over and notice a light on toward the back of the shop. They normally left only a few small lights on the displays near the front window.

"Ben," she said, her voice raspy with sleepiness, "there's a light on in the back. Did you forget?"

"I don't think so," he answered. "But I was in a bit of a hurry when I closed up. I wasn't sure what time you'd all be getting home from shopping."

"Think it'll be okay until the morning?" she asked him.

"I suppose so, but it'd probably be best to go ahead and turn it off. It'll give me a chance to double-check the melters."

"Baby they're on timers, they'll be fine," she yawned.

"I know. I just can't remember if I poured water into the jacketed heaters. It'll just take a minute then I'll get you home."

He parked in back and used his key to unlock the back door that opened up into the alley. "I'll just be a sec," he told her. "Lock the door."

She watched him walk in the door, and leaned her head back into the head rest, lowering the seat a tiny bit to make it a little more comfortable. She had enjoyed the day, but she was ready to go home to Brynn's and get into Ben's warm, comfortable bed. It had begun to feel like home, although they'd been searching for a place of their own.

She adjusted the radio station and turned it down. She glanced back at the door to the shop, expecting Ben to step out any second. When he didn't, she fussed under her breath, thinking he must have found something he'd forgotten to do and gotten quickly absorbed in finishing it. It was just like him to lose track of time.

She stepped out of his SUV, slamming the door shut behind her. When she entered the back room of the shop, she noticed the light was out in the work area. She pinched her brows together, thinking it was odd that he'd already turned off the light but hadn't come out yet. "Ben?" she called out and got no response.

When she rounded the corner from Brynn's old office, the workroom was dark. "Ben?" she repeated. "What are you doing?"

Just then a small light flicked on, light beaming out from the end of a flashlight. The voice she heard chilled her blood.

"He's a bit tied up at the moment," Eric said, and then gave a sinister laugh. The flashlight beam pointed to Ben, who was sitting against a display case with his hands tied to it. His mouth was gagged. His eyes darted rapidly to Ludie, but he couldn't speak.

She gasped, racing toward him.

"I wouldn't do that if I were you," said Eric. "It could be dangerous."

She stopped dead in her tracks. "What are you doing, Eric? Why are you doing this?" Icy fear gripped her heart, her belly rocked by a series of small spasms.

"The question is," he answered, glaring at her belly, "why are you letting this man near my child? Is there nothing sacred to you?"

"*Your* child?" she asked, incredulous. "What are you talking about? I lost your child nearly a year ago. I've moved on with my life, and Ben and I are having a baby."

He slammed his fist down on a table, knocking a slab of wax and some glass jars off the edge and onto the floor where they shattered promptly. "A year ago? You're a horrible liar, Amigo. It was just a few weeks ago you told me about our baby, and I've wanted nothing more than to be with you." He raked his eyes slowly over her swollen belly, now nearly full-term.

She watched as his face clouded over in confusion. Her eyes had adjusted to the light, and she was now able to make out the light reflecting on the steel pistol he held in his hand. She focused on his face, and saw the perplexed expression of an unbalanced man. He seemed so sure of what he was saying, his expression changing rapidly from the joy of an expectant father to the controlled rage of psychosis.

"Eric, you're wrong. You've got to let Ben go. Untie him and we'll leave, no police involved, and we can go our separate ways." She looked over at Ben, barely able to make out his face in the dark shadows. She didn't think he'd be able to break away from the shelves. It was heavy-duty shelving, bracketed to the walls to create enough durability and strength to hold heavy fifty-five pound cases of wax. There were dozens of cases. If he was even able to pull free from the shelving, he'd likely pull it completely over, causing hundreds of pounds of wax blocks to tumble over on him. Sheer panic swept through her. Eric coughed, drawing her attention back to him.

He hadn't taken his eyes off her. He was confident he'd managed to secure Ben well enough to prevent his escape. "Darling you need to stop worrying over your friend. We won't be bothered with him ever again. You and I will be well on the road to our new life together, long before anyone discovers candle boy and his attachment to his work." He gave a sinister laugh, and then seemed disappointed when Ludie didn't find the humor in his joke.

"I'm not going anywhere with you, Eric," she said, bitterness in her voice. "I'm staying with Ben."

"No," he laughed, and began pacing, his gun still in his hand. "I think you're not. You'll come with me, and you'll be quiet, like a good girl. If you don't come quietly, I'm afraid your friend here will get hurt. Cooperate with me, Amigo, and no one has to suffer. This time next week you'll be with me, enjoying our new life. I've already got all the plans drawn out for the nursery. Once we find a place to live, away from all this drama, I'll create the most beautiful nursery you've ever seen."

Ludie eyed him carefully, barely able to make out his features as he emerged yet again from the shadows. *Dear God,* she thought. *He believes all this.*

Looking over at Ben, she gave him an expression that told him she had an idea, and to go along with her. She was amazed at how in-

Donna R Brown

synch the two of them could be. He nodded, careful not to be observed by Eric, who was still pacing and describing the nursery he would create for his 'son,' occasionally being interrupted by small fits of coughing. Ludie remembered how he rarely spent more than a few minutes at a time in the shop because he was unable to tolerate the heavy fragrances for very long. The times he had visited her, he'd ended up having to take puffs from the inhaler he kept in his car. *His car,* she thought. Where was it?

She recalled his aversion to heavy scents, and a night when he'd come home to find her burning a candle she'd made at work. It sat on the bar, flickering away, and she had thought it was lovely. Eric responded furiously, warning her to never bring home another candle with cinnamon in it. He was terribly allergic, he told her, and she quickly extinguished it and took it outside, where she'd gone to retrieve his inhaler from his car.

Her plan was solidifying in her mind, and again she looked over at Ben, careful not to be seen. She flashed an intense stare, and he knew immediately that she had an idea.

"Eric," she said slowly. "How can I be sure you're telling me the truth? You say you want to be with me, but I remember when I first told you about the baby. You were so angry."

"Oh, sweetheart, no, not anymore. I was just surprised, that's all." He looked over at her, his eyes filled with emotion. "I will never reject you, or our son." As he spoke, intensity sharpened his features.

"I hope you're telling me the truth," she said, hoping he wouldn't be able to detect the tremors in her voice. "I can't imagine having my heart broken again."

Looking pointedly over at the melting pot, she clicked her tongue. "He can't do *anything* right," she said. "Ben, you didn't even have this wax at the right temperature." She was grateful for the timer system and thermostats that ensured they'd come in each morning to find wax at the right temperature for pouring.

"It'll all be ruined," she said. Eric laughed at him, calling him candle boy again and telling him he was a failure even at that.

"I always have to fix everything," she laughed, looking over at Eric. "Let me move some of this to the other melting pot and then we'll go."

"No," Eric said, "we need to go now. Besides, why do you care what happens to his candles? It was his carelessness, he can deal with it."

"I care about Brynn." She smiled over at Eric. "Besides, just because he doesn't take any pride in his work, doesn't mean I don't. Just let me transfer this wax and we can go."

He seemed hesitant at first, then smiled back at her, and told her he was proud of her for being so good at her little job. "Hurry," he ordered.

She reached over and began dispensing wax from the large melting pot into a smaller mixing vat. She turned up the temperature gauge and waited for it to hit the right point. Looking at the bottles of oil, she reached up and grabbed one labeled "*pure cinnamon oil*," and poured it in, quickly returning it to the shelf before he realized what she had added. The fragrance quickly blended and began to fill the air with heavy fumes. She had added a significantly larger amount of oil than was called for in that amount of wax.

It wasn't long before Eric was overcome by a fit of coughing and began wheezing. He was bent over near the counter, holding on to the edge to brace himself. Ludie looked over at Ben, who had realized what she was doing and nodded to let her know he understood her plan.

Ludie was waiting for Eric to become so overcome by the fumes that he'd need to go to find his car and retrieve his inhaler. She was horrified when he reached into his pocket and removed it, taking a long puff. Breathing in deeply, he stepped over to the melting pot and placed a heavy lid on the vat and turned it off. Still brandishing the gun, he shook his head slowly and turned back to look at her.

"Bravo," he said, and clicked his tongue in disapproval. "Nice work," he said. "I would be proud of you for having enough brain cells to concoct such a scheme if I weren't so disgusted by your lies. You make me sick."

He waved his gun, gesturing toward Ben, indicating the shelving units where he was tied. "Over there," he barked. "And just remember, you did this to yourself. You wanted to be with him *so badly*."

"Now, I'm just going to waltz out of here,"

he continued as he tied her wrists. "And you're going to stay in here with your *lover*," he hissed. When he had her sufficiently restrained, he placed a gag over her mouth as well. "But before I go, I thought I would do something nice for the lovers. What would romance be without candles?"

He turned up the temperature gauge on the melting pots and poured some pitchers of wax and oils in as he'd seen Ludie do moments earlier. Adding bottle after bottle of fragrance oils, he turned and glared at them.

"By the time anyone finds you two burning the candle at both ends, I'll be long gone." Again he laughed at his own joke, and turned back to them. "But then again, so will both of you."

"Ah, there's nothing like a lovely candle to set the mood, is there, Luv?" spoke a voice in the doorway. Roxy stood behind Dennis, who held a gun in his hand. Eric had amazingly let his guard down while he carried out his plans.

"Drop the gun, Butler," ordered Dennis. "The police are on their way."

Eric made one last move to regain control, and a shot rang out, piercing the air and punctuating Dennis's words. Roxy flipped the lights on to reveal Eric gripping his arm. Blood spread quickly down his sleeve, and he grimaced at the sound of his pistol hitting the floor.

The air was growing heavier and cloudier by the second as the vats of melted wax reached dangerous temperatures. The two smoke alarms rang out, staggered by a split second, echoing each other in turn. Dennis had snatched Eric's gun from the floor and was rapidly cutting the ropes that secured Ludie and Ben to the shelving units while Roxy quickly unplugged the heated pots and covered the wax, helping to reduce the smoke that filled the air.

Eric lay on the floor, his blood rapidly spilling into a sticky growing pool on the floor. He was on the floor, coughing and moaning in agony. Once Ben and Ludie were free, Dennis and Roxy helped them to their feet and led them to the door out into the alley. Ludie couldn't afford to risk another moment exposed to the smoke that hung heavily in the air.

Sirens screamed out into the dark night, growing louder as they drew closer. Ludie looked at Roxy, her eyes forming questions she was unable to ask.

"We were coming home late," Roxy told her. "Don't judge me, we were just out for a drive," she snapped. "When we passed in front of the shop we saw a bit of light reflecting in the displays and there was smoke in the air. We drove 'round back and saw Ben's car. Dennis and I came through the back door and heard what was going on."

Just then Owen, the fire chief, pulled up in his red department-issued truck, with the fire engine not far behind him. His men made quick work of entering the building and taking hold of the situation. Certain that they had it under control, they brought a bleeding, wheezing Eric out into the alley.

Two police cars pulled in from the other

direction, screeching to a halt in the alley. Owen shoved Eric forward, and the officers went for him immediately. "Blackwater to medic one," one of the officers said, squeezing the side of the radio attached to his uniform at the shoulder. "We've got one injury and one that needs to be evaluated."

Ludie was led to the back of a car and assisted to take a seat. "We just need them to check you out and make sure you're all right, under the circumstances," the officer told her. "A woman in your condition needs to be careful."

Eric was bent over the trunk of a police car with an officer on each side. One was reading him his rights, and the other followed by telling him he would be checked out by a medic and treated at the hospital. "As soon as you're released," he told him, "you're mine for a while. Apparently you have a flight to catch before long. Much as I wish we could deal with you here, apparently the DA in Chicago called dibs to get you first, so you've got to be extradited. You've got some bigger charges to face there first, I guess."

At this, Ludie shivered, wondering what the charges could be to make them worse than what he'd done here.

Dennis was standing over Eric and telling him how he really would be much better off in Chicago. "You made a poor choice when you came down to Texas," he was saying. "And you were downright stupid when you set your mind on coming to Blackwater. Haven't you ever learned not to mess with Texas?" he asked him. "We take care of our own, you remember that." Eric's face twisted in despair.

Ludie looked up at Ben, who was anxiously watching for an ambulance. "Just take some deep breaths, honey," he said, rubbing her hand. "It's going to be okay." She waited for him to finish speaking.

"I love you," she said, "and I know it's going to be okay."

"I love you too, baby," he said to her. "And I'm so glad you chose me, and agreed to spend your life with me."

He bent down and kissed her gently, placing his hand on her belly. "Annie, it's your Daddy talking. You and your Mommy and I are going to start a beautiful life together. As soon as Mommy learns that Daddy has been making candles much longer than her." He looked back up at Ludie and, with a teasing look on his face asked, "Now what were you saying about how I leave the melting pots?"

"I'll tell you all about it," she laughed. "But you might want to get some paper so you can take notes. You've got a lot to learn."


The End.